'Max. What do you want?' she demanded rudely.

'Coffee, thanks,' he replied briskly. 'Black. One sugar.' He dropped down into one of the comfortable armchairs.

Abby frowned. 'I wasn't offering you anything to drink,' she told him impatiently.

'No?' He raised dark brows, his grey gaze moving slowly over her face before moving down to her slender curves in denim and a blue T-shirt. 'What were you offering me, then?'

Carole Mortimer was born in England, the youngest of three children. She began writing in 1978, and has now written over one hundred and twenty-five books for Harlequin Mills & Boon®. Carole has four sons—Matthew, Joshua, Timothy and Peter—and a bearded collie dog called Merlyn. She says, 'I'm in a very happy relationship with Peter Senior; we're best friends as well as lovers, which is probably the best recipe for a successful relationship.'

Recent titles by the same author:

The Prince Brothers trilogy

PRINCE'S PASSION
PRINCE'S PLEASURE
PRINCE'S LOVE-CHILD

THE INNOCENT VIRGIN

BY
CAROLE MORTIMER

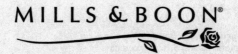

MILLS & BOON®

First published in Great Britain 2006
Harlequin Mills & Boon Limited,
Eton House, 18-24 Paradise Road, Richmond, Surrey TW9 1SR

© Carole Mortimer 2006

ISBN 0 263 84814 0

Set in Times Roman 10½ on 12¼ pt.
01-0506-48127

Printed and bound in Spain
by Litografia Rosés, S.A., Barcelona

CHAPTER ONE

ABBY stepped into the hot scented bathwater, sat down, and let her shoulders sink beneath the luxurious bubbles, ebony hair secured loosely on top of her head, a glass of champagne in one hand, her mobile phone in the other.

She took a large sip from the former before gently dropping the latter into the water beside her, smiling at the satisfying 'glug' it gave before sinking to the bottom without trace. The four-inch layer of bubbles simply closed back over the temporary dent the mobile had made in their formation.

The landline was unplugged, the speaker system from her doorbell in the street downstairs switched off. Nothing and no one was going to disturb this hour of decadence.

She took another sip of the champagne and gazed from the free-standing claw-footed bath at her surroundings. Twelve scented candles were her only illumination and a dreamy smile touched her lips as she looked at her frankly opulent surroundings. The floors and walls were of peach-coloured marble, the glass-sided shower unit that stood at one end of the large room had all its fittings gold-plated; the towels on the racks were a sumptuous peach of the exact shade as the walls and floor. Monty was sitting on the laundry basket, all her bottles of perfume were neatly lined up on the glass shelf beneath the tinted mirror, the bucket of ice containing the bottle of champagne was right beside her, and—

Monty was sitting on the laundry basket!

Her gaze swivelled sharply back to look at him. No, it wasn't the champagne she had already imbibed; Monty really was sitting on top of the laundry basket, unmoving, those green cat-like eyes unblinking.

Well, of course his eyes were cat-like—he was a cat, after all. A huge white, long-haired Persian, to be exact.

Not that Monty was aware of this himself. Somewhere in his youth someone had forgotten to mention this little fact to him, and now he chose to ignore any reference to his species.

Abby wasn't to blame for this oversight; Monty had already been a year old when she'd chosen him over the other cats at the animal rescue centre. At least, she had *thought* she had chosen him; within a very few days of arriving home with him it had become more than obvious that Monty had done the choosing. Someone soft and malleable, he must have decided. Someone still young enough to be moulded into the indulgent, pandering human he needed to make his life completely comfortable. Enter Abby.

'Well, of course that's going to change now, Monty, old chap.' She waved her champagne glass with bravado. 'No more boiled chicken and salmon for you, I'm afraid,' she warned him ruefully. 'From now on you'll be lucky if I can afford to buy you that tinned food you consider so much beneath your notice!'

Cats, she was sure, weren't supposed to be able to

look at you with scepticism and disdain, and yet that was exactly what Monty was doing at this moment. He had several easily readable expressions, from 'You've got to be kidding!' to the smug 'Aren't I lucky to own an accommodating human like Abby?'. At the moment it was definitely the former.

'It isn't my fault,' Abby assured him with another wave of her champagne glass—which definitely needed replenishing, she decided, and did exactly that. 'It's that man's fault.' She took a huge swallow of her champagne. 'I mean, whoever thought he would do such a thing?'

She wouldn't cry. She wouldn't cry!

But of course she did, her tears accompanied by huge, heaving sobs.

How could he have done that to her? And on public television, live, in front of millions of viewers.

Oh, God…!

Every time she even thought of that she felt her humiliation all over again.

'Weeks and weeks—several weeks, anyway,' she amended tearfully. 'Well, okay, seven.' She sniffed inelegantly. 'All that time I've been gently trying to persuade that man to come on my show. Yes, I know you liked him, Monty.' Her voice rose with indignation on her bland-faced pet's behalf. 'So did I,' she admitted heavily. 'But if you only knew—if you had only heard—I had no idea, Monty.' She shuddered. 'Absolutely none!' If she had she would never have got out of bed this morning!

In fact, it was worse than that. If she had guessed in any way just how deep her annihilation was going to be this evening she would have taken a one-way trip to Bolivia earlier today and spared herself all the pain.

She had always liked the sound of that name. Bolivia. It sounded so romantic, so mysterious, so different. But, knowing her luck, it was probably nothing like that at all. She had always liked the sound of the so-called Bermuda Triangle too, but no doubt that was just another myth…

She had probably had too much champagne.

'Okay, okay, so my thoughts are wandering,' she acknowledged, as Monty seemed to look at her with derision. 'But if you only knew, Monty.' She began to cry again, the tears hot on her cheeks. 'If you had only heard what that man said to me! You would have been shocked, Monty. Shocked!'

Abby had actually passed being shocked where this evening was concerned. She had reached surreal now, able to envisage that whole humiliating experience as if in slow motion—like a reel of film going round and round in the projector.

'Oh, God, Monty!' she sobbed. 'I can't ever leave this apartment again! I'll have to barricade the door, put bars on the windows. I daren't ever go out in public again!' She took another slurp of her champagne, the salt of her tears mixing with the bubbly wine. 'Once our supplies run out, we'll both simply starve to death!' she added shakily.

Four months ago it had all looked so promising. As the weather girl for a breakfast television show—an interesting career move, considering she couldn't tell a cold front from an isobar!—she had been asked to stand in for the female half of the presentation team while the other woman went on maternity leave for several months. She had made a impact, and a well-known producer had approached her with an offer to do six half-hour chat shows, to be shown live the following spring.

The next three months had been a dream come true for Abby—choosing the guests for each week, researching, negotiating the appearance of those guests—and everything had gone well until it had come to the guest she had chosen for her final show.

Max Harding.

Her intention had been to finish the series on a high note. Once the presenter of his own current affairs programme, Max Harding had returned to reporting foreign news and hadn't appeared in a British studio in two years. Not since he had walked away from his own programme, and the lucrative contract that went with it, after one of his political guests had tried to commit suicide on the live Sunday evening show.

Max Harding's personal elusiveness since that time, his flat refusal even to discuss the subject, would make him a prime finale, Abby had thought, for her own series of shows.

But she should have known, Abby berated herself now. Should have guessed what his intentions were when he had finally—surprisingly—agreed to be her guest.

'He meant to hurt and humiliate me, Monty.' Her voice hardened angrily at the memory. 'All the time you liked him so much—that I—that we— How could he do that to me, Monty? How could he?' Her ready tears began to fall again. 'But I showed him, Monty. In fact, I showed everyone watching as well,' she remembered with a pained groan. 'Millions and millions of people sat in their homes and watched as I hit him. Yes, you did hear me correctly; I hit Max Harding—on live television!'

Abby closed her eyes as the memory overwhelmed her. She wasn't a violent person—had never hit anyone in her life before, never wanted to hit anyone before. But she had certainly hit Max Harding this evening.

'Actually, it was worse than that, Monty.' She choked, not at all concerned with the fact that a lot of people might think it strange that she was having this conversation with her cat. Temporary insanity was certainly a plea she could make for her actions tonight, but at the moment it was the least of her problems. 'It wasn't just a gentle slap on the cheek.' She groaned. 'He annoyed me so much, hurt me so much, that I swung my arm back and belted him with all the force that I could. It was perfect, Monty. Right on his arrogant chin.' She smiled through her tears with remembered pleasure. 'You should have seen the stunned look on his face. Then his chair toppled backwards, taking him with it, and he was knocked unconscious as he hit the floor!'

And Monty should have seen her own face as her anger had left her and she'd realised exactly what she had done…

The studio had grown so hushed you could literally have heard a pin drop. The small studio audience deathly quiet, no one even seeming to breathe; the camera crew no longer looking into their cameras but staring straight at her in open-mouthed disbelief.

Her director in the control room had been the first to recover, screaming in her earpiece, 'Abby—what the hell are you doing? Say something,' he yelled, when she could only stand there in mute silence, staring down at the slumped form of Max Harding. 'Abby, do something!' Gary had instructed harshly as she still didn't move. 'This is live television, remember?'

She had remembered then, turning to look at the surrounding cameras, realising they were still transmitting.

In her panic there had been only one thing she could do—no other choice left open to her. With a startled cry, she'd stepped over Max Harding's prostrate body before running out of the studio as if pursued.

No one had spoken to her as she'd run. No one had even attempted to stop her.

And why would they? She had totally blown it—had broken the cardinal rule of not losing your cool on public television, of always remaining calm and in control, no matter what the provocation. *No matter what the provocation!*

Her career was in ruins. She would never appear on television ever again.

Which was why she was now locked in her apartment, with the telephone disconnected, the intercom to the doorbell downstairs switched off, and her mobile lying waterlogged in the bottom of the bath.

'Okay, that last gesture may have been a little drastic,' Abby allowed, as Monty looked at her with disapproval. 'Especially as I'm now effectively unemployed—unemployable!—and will never be able to afford to buy a new one. But do you know the worst of it, Monty? The absolute worst of it?' Her voice shook with emotion now, tears once again falling hotly down her cheeks. 'I know you liked him, but I actually thought I was in love with him!' she burst out shakily. 'I was in love with Max Harding!' She whipped herself with the lash again. 'Now I wish I had never even set eyes on him!'

Until seven weeks ago she hadn't even met him.

Seven weeks ago she had been riding on the crest of a wave, euphoric at her success in landing her own half-hour show, full of enthusiasm as she researched and then met her guests, overjoyed at her apparent overnight success at only twenty-seven.

But seven weeks ago Max Harding had still been just a name to her—a reputation, several dozen photographs. She hadn't met the flesh-and-blood man then.

Hadn't fallen in love with him...

CHAPTER TWO

'YES?'

Abby could only stare at the man standing in the open doorway of the apartment; she hadn't seen this much naked male flesh since she'd sat on a beach in Majorca last year.

And very male flesh it was too. But the towel wrapped around the man's slim waist and the dampness of his dark hair told her exactly why it had taken four knocks on the apartment door for him to answer—he had obviously been taking a shower when she arrived.

Alone? Or with someone? Whatever; this man's semi-nakedness took her breath—and her voice—away.

Not that she wasn't familiar with Max Harding's looks. She had seen him dozens of times on the news over the last couple of years, reporting from one war-torn country or another, and had also watched hours of footage of the political forum programme he'd hosted until two years ago.

But in the first case he was usually wearing some sort of combat gear and a flak jacket, shouting his report over the whine of bullets as they whistled past his ears. And in the second instance he had always been sitting down in one of those high-back leather chairs, wearing a dark formal suit with a shirt and tie.

In both cases he had been on the small screen, minimised before being transmitted into people's homes.

He was huge, was Abby's first thought. It wasn't just his height, of about six feet two inches, he also had incredibly wide and muscled shoulders, his skin was darkly tanned, the ebony hair on that powerful chest tapered down to—

'Seen enough?'

Not nearly enough, was her second, slightly fevered thought. *Oh, dear!* was her wincing next one, as she slowly raised her gaze back to his face, her cheeks awash with embarrassed colour.

Really, it might be some time since she had seen a man naked—or in this case semi-naked—but she *had* seen one or two!

But looking at Max Harding's face wasn't reassuring. She had hoped the severity of his expression on television was due to the seriousness of his subject matter, but even one glance at his rock-hewn features was enough to tell her that those weren't laughter lines beside the intense grey eyes, the arrogant slash of a nose and sculptured unsmiling mouth. This man looked as if he rarely smiled, let alone laughed!

Abby straightened her shoulders, deliberately arranging her features into 'serious but pleasant'. 'I don't know if you've heard of me, Mr Harding, but I'm Abby Freeman—'

She didn't get any further than that. The door firmly slammed in her face.

He had heard of her, she thought ruefully. His reaction was a bit drastic, though! Especially as he must have received at least two letters concerning appearing on her show—one from her researchers, and one from her personally. Neither of which he had answered. But he might at least have—

Her eyes widened as the door suddenly swung open again. A hand reached out to grasp the collar of her jacket, and she was unceremoniously pulled inside the apartment, her boot-clad feet barely touching the luxurious carpet.

'Mr Harding—'

'How the hell did you get up here?' He glowered down at her, somehow still managing to look imposing despite his lack of clothing and the wild disorder of his overlong dark hair.

Abby blinked, totally stunned at finding herself inside the apartment instead of outside it.

She delayed answering as she pulled her white T-shirt back into place beneath her black jacket, her ebony hair loose onto her shoulders, blue eyes wide as she fought her inner feelings of indignation.

'I said—'

'The man downstairs let me in,' she cut in.

'After you told him what?' Max Harding bit out contemptuously, hands on narrow hips.

Bare hips, Abby noted somewhat awkwardly. The towel was starting to slip down those long, muscular, hair-covered legs.

'I'm waiting for an explanation, Miss Freeman,' he reminded her harshly, those grey eyes glacial now.

Abby bristled; he sounded like a schoolteacher talking to a disobedient schoolgirl!

'Maybe you should go and put some clothes on?' she suggested with forced pleasantness. 'I'm sure you—' and she! '—would be more comfortable if you did.'

'I'm not uncomfortable, Miss Freeman,' he assured her derisively, enjoying the fact that she obviously was. His mouth hardened before he spoke again. 'Exactly what story did you spin Henry in order to get him to let you up here without first ringing me?'

That cold silver gaze was very forceful, Abby decided with discomfort. The sort of gaze that would compel you to confess to whatever it was this man *wanted* you to confess to, whether you were guilty or not.

She grimaced. 'I told him I was your younger sister, that it's your birthday today, and that I wanted to surprise you,' she answered truthfully.

That sculptured mouth twisted wryly. 'Not bad for a beginner,' he drawled.

Her cheeks flushed. 'Now, look—'

'On your way out,' Max Harding continued, as if she hadn't spoken, 'you can tell him you succeeded.' He opened the door pointedly. 'I'll tell him what I think later!' he added grimly.

Abby didn't move towards the door. Having got this far, she had no intention of leaving just yet. 'I hope not with any idea of reprimand in mind? I can be very persuasive when I try.' She gave him an encouraging smile.

A smile he made no effort to return, and that steely, unamused grey gaze quickly made the smile falter and then fade.

Back to business, she decided hastily. 'I've written to you several times, Mr Harding—'

'Twice, to be exact,' he interrupted, his terse tone telling her that he liked to be that, at least. 'Two letters, both of which I read before duly consigning them to the bin!'

He had enjoyed telling her that, Abby realised with an annoyance she tried hard not to show—one of them being antagonistic was quite enough! Besides, she couldn't afford to be. She had assured the sarcastic and sceptical Gary Holmes, director of *The Abby Freeman Show*, that she would get Max Harding to appear on her final show. A very ambitious claim, she had come to realise over the last few weeks, but she needed something—someone!—really impressive to finish the series if she were to stand any chance of being offered another contract.

Though she did wish she had approached Max Harding before making that ambitious claim to Gary...!

She gave Max Harding a bright, unruffled smile. 'Then you will be aware that the whole of the half-hour show will be dedicated to you—'

'No.'

'Oh, but I'm sure I made that clear in my letter.' Abby frowned. 'I would hardly offer less to a man of your professional stature—'

'Cut the bull, Miss Freeman,' he bit out harshly. 'In this case flattery, professional or otherwise, will get you precisely nowhere! I have no intention, now or ever, of appearing on *The Abby Freeman Show*.' He made the programme title sound like something obscene.

Nevertheless, Abby persevered; this was too important to allow obvious insults to upset her. 'But you're such an interesting man, Mr Harding,' she said lightly. 'You've seen so much, done so much, and I'm sure the general public would be fascinated to hear about—'

'The general public have absolutely no more interest than you do in hearing about any of the things I've seen and done,' he rasped coldly. 'All anyone wants to hear about from me is the night Rory Mayhew tried to commit suicide on my television programme.' His eyes glittered icily. 'It also happens to be the one thing I will never discuss in public. Is that clear enough for you, Miss Freeman?'

Crystal-clear. And he was partly right about the Rory Mayhew 'incident'; obviously it was such a big thing that she could hardly *not* ask about it. But it certainly wasn't the only thing she wanted him to talk about. They could hardly discuss an attempted suicide for the whole of a thirty-minute interview, for goodness' sake.

'I thought about mentioning that initially, obviously,' she conceded. 'But then I thought we could move on to other things. Your last two years as a foreign correspondent have made fascinating listening, and—'

'I said no, Miss Freeman.'

'Oh, please do call me Abby,' she invited, with a warmth she was far from feeling. In fact, the coldness emanating from this man was enough to make her give an involuntary shiver.

'You can call me Mr Harding,' he bit out. 'But first—' he moved to close the door again, its soft click much more ominous than the loud slam of a few minutes ago '—I have one or two questions I would like to put to you.'

The sudden smoothness of his tone was more menacing than his previous sarcasm and coldness, making Abby very aware that she was completely alone in this penthouse apartment with a powerful-looking man. A very angry, half-naked, powerful-looking man!

She gave him another of her bright, confident smiles—although inside she was neither of those things. This meeting with Max Harding wasn't turning out at all as she had hoped. 'Fire away, Mr Harding,' she invited lightly. 'I'm happy to answer any questions you have concerning the programme. In fact, I look on it as a very positive—'

'My questions have absolutely nothing to do with your programme, Miss Freeman,' he assured her scornfully, 'and everything to do with how you obtained my personal address in the first place.' His voice had hardened over this last, his expression grim.

Not much of a chance of him offering her a coffee, then! Or inviting her to sit down in the comfortable lounge she could see through the open doorway behind her.

Not much chance of this turning into a successful meeting, either, if the conversation so far was anything to go by.

'And don't say the local telephone book,' he warned. 'Because I'm ex-directory.'

Her palms were starting to feel slightly damp, and she was sure there was an unbecoming sheen materialising on her top lip.

Nevertheless, she forced another carefree smile to her face. 'The *how* isn't really important—'

'It is to me.' He stood firmly in front of the door now—her only means of escape!—powerfully muscled arms folded in front of that bare chest.

In the same circumstances, wrapped only in a towel, Abby knew that she would feel at a distinct disadvantage talking to anyone. And yet this man gave no such impression—in fact, the opposite. He seemed to know exactly how his near-nakedness was making her feel— and he was enjoying watching her squirm.

Because squirming she undoubtably was. This man, Max Harding, she was becoming increasingly aware, exuded a sexual magnetism that had very little to do with whether or not he was wearing any clothes! There was a toughness to him, a self-containment, that at thirty-nine had been hard earned.

He made a sudden movement, quickly followed by the first sign of amusement, albeit mocking, she had seen on his harsh features. Abby instinctively took a step backwards. 'I don't usually eat little girls like you until after breakfast,' he drawled, grey eyes mocking as he looked her over with slow deliberation. 'You're one of those "bright young things" the powers-that-be in public television have decided the masses want piped into their homes every minute of the day and night, aren't you?'

'I—'

'What did you do before being given *The Abby Freeman Show*?' he continued, unabated. 'Present one of those kids programmes where you have to constantly look like a teenager—even though you're not—and rush around risking life and limb climbing mountains and jumping out of aeroplanes? I'm sorry, what did you say?' he prompted scornfully as Abby muttered something inaudible.

Her chin rose defensively, twin circles of colour in her cheeks. 'I said I was the weather presenter on a breakfast show, and then the stand-in presenter,' she repeated tautly. Withstanding Max Harding's obvious derision certainly hadn't been in her plans for today!

He continued to look at her, his expression blank now, as if he wasn't quite sure he had heard her correctly. And then his mouth twitched and he began to laugh, a harsh, humourless sound that echoed the scorn in his eyes. 'A weather girl?' he finally sobered enough to say disbelievingly.

Her cheeks felt on fire now. 'You don't have a lot of respect for your fellow presenters, do you?'

'On the contrary, Abby, I have *immense* respect for my fellow presenters—you just don't happen to be one!'

This was important to her—very important if she was to prove to Gary Holmes she wasn't the lightweight he insisted on treating her as. But right now, with Max Harding's derision directly in her face, she wanted to turn on her heel and run. Unfortunately, Max Harding still stood between her and the door!

Attack, she was sure, was still the best form of defence. 'I never had you figured for a misogynist, Mr Harding!'

He didn't even grimace at the insult. 'Oh, but I'm not, Abby,' he told her, silkily soft, his grey eyes hooded as he looked her over with slow deliberation from her toes to the top of her ebony head. The arrogantly mocking gaze finally returned to her flushed face and he gave a derisive shake of his head. 'You just aren't my type,' he drawled, with deliberate rudeness.

She should never have come here, Abby realised belatedly. She had thought she was being so clever, fooling Henry downstairs, and had been quietly patting herself on the back at her success all the way up here in the lift. But all she had really succeeded in doing was totally annoying this man. And even on this short an acquaintance she knew he would be dangerous when he was annoyed!

Come to that, he was dangerous when he *wasn't* annoyed. She couldn't imagine what she had been thinking of!

She hadn't really been thinking at all, she finally realized. Had been too stung by Gary Holmes's scornful scepticism that she would ever persuade Max Harding to appear on her show to plan this meeting today any further than actually meeting the man face to face.

'You and my director should meet,' she snapped irritably. 'The two of you have so much in common!'

'Doesn't he like working with amateurs either?' Max Harding taunted.

That was it.

She had had enough.

More than enough!

She had already spent weeks at the sharp end of Gary Holmes's sarcastic tongue; she had no intention of taking it from this man too! Besides, he wasn't going to appear on her show anyway, so she really had nothing to lose!

She drew herself up angrily. 'I have no idea why I ever thought anyone would be interested in hearing any-thing you have to say.' And she didn't—not anymore. 'You're rude. You're arrogant. You're mocking, and thoroughly unpleasant. And I don't like you!' Her hands were clenched into fists at her sides.

Max Harding continued to look at her for several long seconds, and then he gave a decisive nod. 'That, my dear Abby, is the most honest thing you've said all morning! Come on.' He stepped past her into the lounge. 'I'll put some coffee on to brew while I'm dressing.'

Abby stood open-mouthed, watching him as he strolled across the sitting room and into what she as-sumed must be the kitchen.

She had been as rude and brutally frank as he was himself, and now he was offering to make her coffee!

She gave a slightly befuddled shake of her head be-fore following him. She would have given up all pre-tence of politeness long before now if she had known this would be the result.

The sitting room, as she had already observed from the hallway, was spacious and well-furnished, deco-rated in warm, sunny golds and creams, with a wonder-ful view over London from the huge picture window. It also looked totally unlived-in—like a hotel suite, or as if the interior designer had only finished his work yesterday and everything was new and unused.

The kitchen was almost as big, with walnut cupboards and gold-coloured fittings. But apart from the coffee percolator, which had already started its aromatic drip into the pot, the work surfaces were bare—as if this room were rarely used either.

'Take a seat,' Max Harding invited, without turning round as he got coffee mugs from a cupboard.

Abby made herself comfortable on one of the stools at the breakfast bar—well, as comfortable as someone of five foot four could be on one of the high stools!— still not quite sure how she had managed to get herself invited in for coffee. But she wasn't complaining. The less inclined Max Harding was to throw her out, the more chance she had of persuading him to change his mind about appearing on her programme.

'Right.' He turned from what he was doing. 'I'll go and throw on some clothes while the coffee's filtering. Oh, and Abby?' He paused in the kitchen doorway, his expression once again derisive. 'Stay exactly where you are!'

She looked at him blankly for several seconds, frowning, her cheeks becoming hot as she realised what he meant. 'I'm not a snoop, Mr Harding,' she protested waspishly.

His mouth twisted. 'That's why you'll never make an investigative reporter!' he retorted, before leaving the room.

Abby put her elbows on the breakfast bar and leant forward to rub her throbbing temples with her thumbs, wondering if all these insults really were worth it. Even if she succeeded if getting him to appear on the show—

which was doubtful!—there was no way, him being the man that he was, that she was going to be able to control the interview. And that wasn't going to help her get that second contract she wanted. Maybe…

'I didn't mean it quite that literally,' Max remarked scathingly as he came back into the room. 'You could have helped yourself to coffee.'

In truth, she had been so lost in her own thoughts she hadn't really been aware that the coffee had stopped filtering into the pot. And, as she looked up at him now, her mind once again went completely blank.

'I'll go and throw on some clothes' was what he had said, and, looking at him, that was pretty much what he had done. His damp hair looked as if he had just run a hand through it, he was wearing a clean, but very creased white T-shirt, and a pair of ragged denims, also clean, but worn and faded, the bottoms frayed. And that was all he was wearing from what Abby could tell. His feet were bare on the coolness of the tiled floor.

He looked sexy as hell!

This side of Max Harding hadn't really been apparent in the tapes of his shows she had watched from the archives, but she had certainly been made aware of it when he'd opened the door earlier, wearing only a towel. And—strangely—she was even more aware of him now, because the clothes hinted at the powerful body beneath.

She straightened, shaking her head. 'Sorry. It didn't occur to me.'

He placed a steaming mug of black, unsweetened coffee in front of her. 'There isn't any milk,' he announced off-handedly as he passed her the sugar bowl. 'I only got back late last night, and I haven't had time to shop yet.'

'Black is fine,' she assured him, though she usually took both cream and sugar in her beverages. Somehow, from the look of the unused kitchen, she doubted he had time to go to the shops very often!

'So.' He sat down opposite her at the breakfast bar, his gaze piercing. 'You have yet to answer my question.'

She could always try acting dumb and ask which question he was referring to— but as he already thought she was dumb that probably wasn't the approach to take!

She shrugged. 'I obtained your address from a friend of a friend,' she said dismissively, wishing she felt more self-confident and less physically aware of this man...

His gaze narrowed. 'Which friend of what friend?'

'Is that grammatically correct?' She attempted to tease, deciding that probably wasn't a good idea either as his scowl deepened. 'You aren't seriously expecting me to answer that?'

He didn't return her cajoling smile. 'I rarely joke about an invasion of my privacy,' he grated.

She raised ebony brows. 'Aren't you overreacting just a little? After all, I only rang the doorbell. You were the one who invited me in!'

'I can just as easily throw you out again!' he rasped. 'And I "invited" you in as you put it, for the sole purpose of ascertaining how you obtained my address.'

'Knowing full well that I couldn't possibly reveal my source,' Abby came back sharply. Challengingly. It was the first rule of being that investigative reporter he had told her she would never be; a source's identity was as sacrosanct to a reporter as the information a client gave to a lawyer.

Max sat back slightly, his expression—as usual!— unreadable. 'Tell me, Abby,' he said softly, 'just what made you think you would succeed where so many others have failed?'

She blinked, not sure she quite understood the question. Surely he didn't think that she trying to attract—?

'Not that, Abby.' He sighed. 'I was actually referring to other requests for me to appear on TV programmes or give personal interviews to newspapers over the last two years. Haven't I already assured you that you aren't my type?' His mouth twisted scathingly as his gaze raked over her ebony hair, deep blue eyes, creamy complexion and full, pouting lips.

Exactly what was 'his type'? Abby felt like asking, but didn't. As far as her research was concerned, he didn't appear to have a type. He had been married once, in his twenties, and amicably divorced only three years later, and the assortment of women he had been involved with over the years since that marriage didn't seem to fit into any type either, having ranged from hard-hitting businesswomen to a pampered Californian divorcee. The only thing those women seemed to have in common was independence. And possibly an aversion to marriage…?

'Well, that's something positive, at least,' Abby came back dismissively. 'Because you aren't my type either!'

Grudging amusement slightly lightened his expression. 'No,' he murmured thoughtfully. 'I should imagine a nice, safe executive of some kind, preferably in television, would be more your cup of tea.'

This man managed to make everything he said sound insulting!

And in this case he was wrong; she had been briefly engaged to a 'nice, safe executive of some kind'—and been totally bored by Andrew's complete lack of imagination. Besides, Monty hadn't liked him…

'Really?' she said wearily. 'How interesting.'

Max continued to look at her for several seconds, and then gave an appreciative grin. 'You sound like my mother when confronted by one of my father's more boring business associates!'

His father, Abby knew, was James Harding, the owner of Harding Industries. His charming and beautiful wife Amy was a banking heiress, and Max's mother. Obviously Max hadn't inherited that first trait of hers!

'Really?' Abby repeated unhelpfully, slightly disturbed by the attraction of that grin—and desperate not to show it.

'*Really?*' he mimicked dryly. 'Am I boring you, Abby?'

So far she hadn't been able to relax enough in this man's company to feel bored! But if he wanted to think that—fine; she needed every advantage she could get with this thoroughly disconcerting man. 'Not specifically,' she drawled, sounding uninterested.

His mouth quirked humorously. 'How about unspecifically?'

She pretended to give the idea some thought. In fact, she very much doubted too many people found this man boring; the level of mental alertness necessary just to have a conversation with him wouldn't allow for that. Besides, the man was playing with her, and, despite what he might think to the contrary, she really wasn't one of those vacuous 'young things' he had initially accused her of being. At least, she hoped she wasn't!

She had left school with straight As and gone on to graduate from university three years later with a degree in politics. But two years of working as a very junior underling to a politician who just wasn't going to make it, despite putting in sixteen-hour days, had very soon quashed her own ambitions in that direction, and she had done a complete about-face, becoming interested in a career in television instead.

Being the smiling face of a lowbrow programme's weather segment hadn't exactly stretched her mentally, but everyone had to start somewhere. Besides, being offered her own six-week series of interviews now was worth the year she had spent getting up at four-thirty in the morning just so that she could be at the studio bright and early to give her first weather report of the day when the programme began at six-thirty.

And even Max Harding, despite his privileged background and a father who had probably been able to pull a few strings for him, had to have started somewhere—

'Sorry?' She shook her head as she realised Max had just spoken to her.

'I asked whether your meteoric rise to fame has had something to do with the way you look rather than any real qualifications to do the job?' He looked at her challengingly.

He had obviously decided to make sure there was no possible chance of her being bored by him any longer!

But if his intention was to anger her by the obvious insult, then he hadn't succeeded in doing that either. She had heard every insult there was these last two months, from other women as well as men, and especially from Gary Holmes, and she was no longer shocked or bothered by them. Well…not much, anyway.

She gave him a pitying glance. 'Which one do you think I slept with? The producer or the director?'

Grudging respect darkened his eyes. 'Either. Or possibly both.' He shrugged.

Now he wasn't *trying* to be insulting—he was succeeding! 'Pat Connelly is a grandmother several times over, I believe, and seriously not my type!' Abby told him derisively. 'And Gary Holmes is just an obnoxious little creep!' she added with feeling.

A veteran director of fifteen years plus, Gary was one of the most handsome men Abby had ever met—but he had the infuriating habit of treating her like an idiot. He obviously disliked her—possibly because he also thought she was a pretty airhead—but as the dislike was wholly reciprocated Abby wasn't particularly bothered by his attitude. Except on a professional level. And he had hardly given her time to prove—

She suddenly realised that Max had gone strangely quiet, and looked across at him curiously, but she was able to learn nothing from his closed expression. 'What is it?' she prompted with a frown.

He seemed to snap himself out of that scowling silence with effort. 'Nothing,' he said abruptly. 'And if it's taken you this long to think about my previous question, perhaps you would be wiser not to answer at all!' he drawled, with some of his earlier mockery. 'Who's scheduled to appear on your first programme?'

She was a little stunned by this abrupt *volte face*, and would have liked to pursue the reason for his sudden silence, but the coldness in his gaze was enough to warn her that she would get precisely nowhere if she did.

'Natalie West and Brad Hammond,' she answered instead, with not a little pride.

The famous couple, both having appeared on prime-time television, but in different series, had been involved in the very noisy and very public break-up of their marriage six months ago, culminating with Natalie announcing it would give her great pleasure to see Brad run over with a steamroller, and Brad retaliating with the claim that he would gladly step in the path of the steamroller if it meant he didn't have to set eyes on Natalie ever again!

It had taken weeks of persuasion and negotiation on Abby's part, but she had finally got them both to agree—separately—to appear together on her opening programme. It promised to be an explosive debut for *The Abby Freeman Show*!

Max whistled softly through his teeth. 'Are you going to supply the steamroller?'

He did have a sense of humour after all! He also, despite his many career-related trips out of the country, obviously kept up with the less serious side of current affairs.

Abby shook her head, her hair silky against her cheeks, blue eyes gleaming with laughter. 'I already checked—even if Natalie felt so inclined, a steamroller wouldn't fit through the studio door!'

Max gave an appreciative chuckle. 'Perhaps you aren't such a lightweight after all!'

It was far from an apology for his earlier rudeness— in fact it was still a remark tinged with condescension— but it was certainly an improvement on his initial antagonism. 'Does that mean you'll reconsider appearing on my programme?' God, how it still gave her a thrill of pleasure to say 'my programme'!

She had earned a certain amount of recognition from her appearances on breakfast television, with members of the public coming up to her in supermarkets and restaurants to say hello, but she was really hoping that having her own programme was going to take her one step further than that, and earn her the professional respect of people like Max Harding. If she ever got the chance, that was!

'Not in the least.' He instantly shot her down, his tone bored and noncommittal. And totally uncompromising. 'And, as you aren't going to tell me who this "friend of a friend" is…' He raised dark brows.

'I told you I can't do that,' she confirmed, her disappointment acute at his continued refusal.

Max shrugged. 'Then it would appear we have nothing else to say to each other.' He stood up, removing his own empty coffee mug and Abby's full one and placing them on the worktop before turning to look at her pointedly.

He was obviously waiting for her to leave.

She had lied her way up here in the first place, and been taken in to this man's inner sanctum, yet still she had failed in her objective. But other than continuing to pressure him—something guaranteed to annoy him even further—she didn't have any choice but to comply with his less than subtle hint.

'You won't be too hard on Henry?' she asked as she followed Max back through the sitting room to the door. She hadn't realised earlier just how strongly Max felt about any invasion of his privacy, and Henry was a man of advanced years, who would have great difficulty finding another job if he was sacked from this one.

Max glanced back at her. 'Calm down, Abby,' he taunted. 'Having witnessed your persuasive powers firsthand—no, I won't be hard on Henry at all.' He opened the door as he spoke.

Her 'persuasive powers'? Did she have some of those? And if she did, why hadn't Max Harding been persuaded?

He shook his head, smiling slightly. 'Don't beat yourself up trying to work out what they are, Abby; all that matters is that they didn't work on me!'

Obviously not—but she would still have liked to know what they were. If she did, she might be able to use them again—to better effect!

But she could see by the derisive expression on Max's face as he stood there waiting for her to leave that he certainly wasn't going to enlighten her. Pity.

'I'll make a point of watching your first programme,' he told Abby softly as she stepped out into the hallway.

She stared up at him suspiciously, uncertain of exactly what he had meant by that, and unable to read any of his thoughts from his blandly mocking expression.

But he had just succeeded in increasing her own first-night nerves by one hundred per cent!

CHAPTER THREE

'Well, well, if it isn't little Abby Freeman!'

Abby groaned as she sank further down into her armchair, having instantly recognised Max Harding's mocking voice.

Holed up in a corner of the Dillmans' crowded drawing room, having already drunk three-quarters of the bottle of champagne sitting in the ice bucket on the low table beside her, she was in no mood for company. Something everyone else in the room, including her hosts Dorothy and Paul, seemed to know instinctively and act upon—and of which Max Harding had taken no notice whatsoever!

'Go away,' she muttered, without so much as glancing in his direction. She could see the long length of his legs from the corner of her eye, though, and observed that he didn't move by so much as an inch.

'I didn't have you figured as a woman who likes to drink alone.' He sounded amused now.

Abby raised dark lashes in order to glare at him, her gaze belligerent. 'I don't usually drink—alone or otherwise,' she snapped impatiently. 'But I'm sure that you and probably everyone else in this room are aware of the reason I've made tonight the exception.' And several million other people, she thought with another inner groan at the remembered humiliation.

How could she have known? How could she have guessed? Why hadn't someone told her?

'Hey, Abby, it really wasn't that bad.' Max came down on his haunches beside her chair now, the amusement having disappeared from his voice as he looked at her with something like concern. 'In fact, I thought you recovered very well.'

She hadn't 'recovered' well at all, and she was sure that everyone watching the airing of her first show earlier this evening had known it, too.

As previously agreed, she had interviewed Brad Hammond first for ten minutes, chatting warmly about his earlier career and his success now in a popular television series. Then Brad had gone off the set and Natalie had come on for her allotted ten minutes, discussing her own success.

But all the time those interviews were taking place a buzz had been felt in the studio. Both crew and audience obviously waiting expectantly for the time the estranged pair would come on together, with the promise of emotional fireworks in the air.

Except it had turned out Brad and Natalie were no longer estranged!

Abby had announced the two of them coming on together, feeling the tension rising in the studio as she did so, and could have collapsed in a heap when, instead of showing antagonism, Brad and Natalie had smiled warmly at each other before kissing and sitting down close together, their hands entwined, as Brad announced that the two of them had been reconciled for three days.

Abby had been rendered speechless by the announcement. All her carefully prepared questions had become null and void—questions she had spent hours labouring over in an effort to ensure she wouldn't become the cause of further antagonism between the separated couple, intending to leave it to the two of them to set their own scene with as little prompting from her as possible. Brad's announcement had made a complete nonsense of them.

She'd done her best to rally round at this sudden change of circumstances, congratulating them on their reconciliation, asking what their plans were for the future. A *baby*, for goodness' sake; after all the public insults they had hurled at each other over the last six months!

Yes, Abby had done her best to keep the show alive and buzzing, but she had been aware that it had definitely lacked the sparkle and interest she had been hoping for when she'd invited the pair on her show.

And Gary Holmes's snort of derision when she'd finally walked off the set had been enough to send her hurtling for the champagne bottle the moment she'd reached Dorothy and Paul's house half an hour ago.

'Go away,' she told Max Harding a second time, turning away to lift up the champagne bottle, having no intention of crossing swords with him this evening.

Instead of complying with her request, she felt him take the champagne bottle from her hand. Her grip tightened but was no match for Max's superior strength. The fluted champagne glass in her other hand was the next to go, before Max took her by one of her now empty hands and pulled her effortlessly to her feet.

'You need food,' he told her firmly as she began to

protest. 'Otherwise the headlines on tomorrow's tab-
loids will read "Abby Freeman plastered", accompanied
by a photograph of you being carried out of here!' He
didn't wait for any more arguments as he tucked her
hand into the crook of his arm and guided her into the
adjoining room, where a table was set with a sumptuous buffet supper.

Not that Abby had been about to argue with him; the
way she'd swayed unsteadily as she got to her feet, with
the room tilting dizzily, was enough to tell her that food
was exactly what she needed. Even if it was the last
thing she *wanted!*

'There you go.' Max placed a heavily laden plate in
her unresisting hand before turning to choose some food
for himself.

Abby's vision blurred as she looked down at the food.
'Why are you being so nice to me?' She sniffed, not sure
she was going to be able to hold back the tears for much
longer, despite blinking them away desperately.

He glanced at her, very tall and handsome in a black
evening suit and snowy white shirt, although the dark
hair was even longer than it had been when they'd met
three weeks ago, and the grey eyes were still as mockingly amused.

'I figured someone ought to be,' he drawled dismissively. 'You presented rather a lonely figure sitting in
there.' He nodded in the direction of the drawing room.

Pity. He felt sorry for her. And only hours ago she had
hoped to finish this evening on a note of triumph.
Euphoria, even.

'Keep your damned pity!' she snapped as she
slammed the untouched plate of food back down on the
table, her eyes sparkling deeply blue, twin spots of

angry colour in her cheeks. 'You've heard of the phoenix rising from the ashes? Well, watch the show next week and see what a good job I make of doing exactly that!' She turned on her heel and walked—steadily, thank goodness!—out of the room, unknowingly beautiful in her midnight-blue knee-length dress, dark hair loose about her shoulders. She made her way over to where she could see Dorothy, chatting with a well-known newspaper reporter.

Dorothy's parties were always like this—attended by the rich and the famous—although Dorothy herself was one of the least glamorous people Abby knew. Her plain black evening gown was an old favourite with her, her face was homely rather than beautiful, and her figure tended towards comfortable plumpness now that she was approaching her sixtieth year.

But Abby had known the other woman all her life—knew that it was Dorothy's genuine warmth and kindness that attracted people to her like a magnet. Her handsome husband of the last thirty-five years absolutely adored her.

'You can't leave just yet, Abby!' Dorothy responded with genuine regret at Abby's excuse of tiredness. 'I haven't had a chance to introduce you to anyone,' she protested. 'Jenny and I were just commenting on what an absolute triumph your programme was this evening. Natalie and Brad have made complete idiots of themselves these last few months, and I don't think there was a dry eye in the house—well, certainly not in this one!' she admitted unabashedly '—when they announced that they're back together and trying for a baby.'

Abby's smile was fixed on her face with sickening determination. She knew Dorothy was only trying to be kind by talking like that about her show—the older woman didn't know how to be anything else!—but Abby really wished she didn't have to stand here and listen to this. The whole show had been a disaster as far as she was concerned—and as far as Gary Holmes was, too, if his scornful remarks as she'd left the studio were anything to go by.

'Yes.' Jenny Jones took over the conversation, her manner slightly gushing. 'The Natalie and Brad reconciliation was an absolute coup for your first programme!'

Was it? Or was the other woman just veiling her sarcasm for Dorothy's benefit?

No, Abby realized, slightly dazedly, Jenny Jones looked genuinely disappointed that *she* hadn't been the one to scoop the exclusive.

Abby brightened. Maybe it hadn't been such a disaster, after all? Meaning that perhaps Max's earlier comments hadn't been out of the pity that she had thought they were either?

No—there was no need to go that far! If her show *hadn't* been the complete failure she had initially thought it was, then she still knew she had only scraped through by the skin of her teeth, and someone as acutely intelligent as Max would be aware of that fact, too. And she would rather listen to Dorothy and Jenny's misplaced praise, than Max's mocking condescension.

'My editor is running the story on the front page tomorrow,' Jenny confided. '"Abby Shock: Brad No Longer a Free Man!"'

Abby gave a pained wince at the awful play on her surname. Although she couldn't really have expected much else from the dreadful rag Jenny worked for. But she didn't think Natalie would care for the headline too much, either!

'How clever,' Dorothy put in lightly at the lengthening silence. 'I do so wish I could think of things like that.'

'It comes with experience,' Jenny consoled her slightly pityingly as she laid a sympathetic hand on the other woman's arm. 'I— Oh, look, there's Max Harding.' Her green eyes were bright with the fervour of the predator as she spotted Max entering the room. 'I've been wanting to speak to him for absolutely ages. If you ladies would excuse me…?' she added distractedly, not waiting for either of them to reply before striding purposefully across the room in Max Harding's direction.

'Gladly!' Dorothy muttered with feeling. 'That woman is such a pompous bore!' she added with disdain.

'Dorothy…?' Abby looked at the older woman incredulously. 'I've never heard you say an unkind word about anyone before,' she explained at Dorothy's questioning look.

'No? Well, put it down to my age.' Dorothy chuckled, easily shrugging off her brief bad humour. 'My only consolation is that I know Max will quickly send her away with a flea in her ear! There.' She nodded with satisfaction as she glanced across the room. 'That has to be something of a record—even for Max.' She sounded impressed.

Abby turned just in time to see Jenny Jones beating a hasty retreat from the glacially angry Max. There were twin spots of humiliated colour in the tabloid reporter's cheeks. Having received what Abby was sure was a similar put-down herself only three weeks ago, she couldn't help but feel a certain fleeting sympathy for the other woman.

'Why does he do that?' she mused, shaking her head as she turned back to look at Dorothy. 'And get away with it, too!' she added wryly, absolutely positive that not a single word of Max's rude put-down of the other woman would ever reach the pages of even the tacky tabloid Jenny worked for.

'Because he's absolutely brilliant at what he does, of course,' Dorothy answered. 'And gorgeous as hell, too,' she added with relish.

Abby watched as Max fell into easy conversation with Dorothy's husband Paul. The two men were of similar height and build. Paul's blond hair was sprinkled liberally with grey, but otherwise, to Abby's eyes, he looked every bit as fit and handsome as the younger man.

'I would rather have Paul any day,' she announced firmly.

'Well, of course, having been married to the darling man for thirty-five years, so would I,' Dorothy agreed laughingly. 'But that doesn't mean I'm blind to the way other men look—and Max has to be the epitome of "tall, dark and handsome". And all that brooding aloofness has to be a direct challenge to any normal red-blooded woman!'

Then Abby had to be an *abnormal* red-blooded woman—because she had been daunted by Max rather than attracted to him.

Well…she had been attracted to him too—but the daunting had definitely outweighed that attraction!

'If you like that sort of thing,' she dismissed, with an audible sniff of uninterest.

Dorothy gave her a searching look, warm blue eyes probing now. 'You never did tell me how your meeting with him went three weeks ago…?'

Abby withstood that searching gaze for several long seconds before looking away. 'I told you—he said no to coming on the show,' she said with a casual shrug.

'Yes, but—'

'Dorothy, I really don't want to talk about Max Harding.'

'I'm glad to hear it,' he drawled mockingly from directly behind her, making Abby start guiltily. His grey eyes were openly laughing as she turned sharply to face him. 'I find the subject of me boring, too,' he acknowledged, with a derisive inclination of his dark head.

'Then at least we're agreed on something, Mr Harding!' she came back waspishly, completely disconcerted at having him appear behind her in this way; the last time she had looked he had been deep in conversation with Paul.

'Well, well.' Dorothy chuckled with delight. 'What do you have to say to that, Max?' she teased, obviously deeply amused by the turn in conversation.

Max gave the older woman an affectionate smile. 'That Abby obviously has exceptional taste,' he drawled unconcernedly. 'Here.' He handed Abby one of the two champagne flutes he held in his hands. 'I thought you might be in need of it after talking to Jenny Jones!' He grimaced.

'What a perfectly dreadful woman,' Dorothy agreed as Abby rather dazedly took the glass of bubbly wine from Max. 'I really will have to have a chat with Paul about the sort of people he's inviting into our home. In fact, if the two of you will excuse me, I think I'll just go and have a word with him now.' She gave them a bright smile before moving to join her husband.

Leaving Abby completely alone with Max Harding. Again. And, despite the champagne she had consumed earlier, she now felt completely sober. Stone-cold sober.

'How is it that you know the Dillmans so well?' Max asked lightly.

'As until quite recently I was only a lowly weather girl, you mean?' she came back tartly.

He took a leisurely sip of his champagne, that grey gaze unwavering as it met Abby's seething eyes. 'I didn't say that,' he finally drawled.

'You didn't need to. But it just so happens that I've known the Dillmans all my life,' she told him with satisfaction.

'Really?' Max murmured, his gaze speculative as he glanced across to where Dorothy was now in laughing conversation with her husband. '"A friend of a friend", I believe you said…?' That grey gaze was once again fixed piercingly on Abby.

Damn it! She was sure Max had just set a trap for her—and she had just walked straight into it. Like an innocent mouse into the lion's den. But unfortunately she seemed to have taken Dorothy in with her, and the other woman deserved better than that.

'That description hardly fits Dorothy,' Abby told him. 'She happens to be my godmother.' Dorothy *was* actually the 'friend of a friend' who had told her Max's home address, but Abby had no intention of betraying her godmother's confidence by admitting that.

'Your godmother?' Max repeated evenly, seeming to be having trouble digesting this piece of information.

'Yes—godmother,' Abby confirmed, wondering what he found so strange about that. 'She and my mother were at school together, and they have remained friends ever since,' she added defensively, wondering just what his problem was with that. Although, whatever it was, it had at least succeeded in diverting his attention away from that 'friend of a friend' she had unwisely admitted three weeks ago to have been the source of his address.

She wasn't quite prepared for what he did next. She was sure her comment hadn't warranted derisive laughter!

But laughter was a definite improvement on his usual mocking expression. Laughter lines appeared beside his eyes and mouth, his teeth were very white and even, and he had a slight dimple in the groove of one cheek.

But none of that detracted from the fact she had no idea what she had said that was so amusing.

'So you were telling the truth after all about your producer and director?' he finally taunted, once his laughter had faded. 'It was relatives in high places instead,' he added appreciatively. 'Oh, don't worry, Abby, I'm not knocking it,' he went on, at her startled and indignant expression. 'We all have to start somewhere, and why not use the advantages—the less obvious ones—' he gave her slender attractiveness in the midnight-blue dress an appreciative glance '—that you have at your disposal.'

It didn't matter that Abby had no idea what he was talking about. His mocking tone and derisive expression were enough to tell her it was nothing pleasant. But then 'pleasant' hardly described this man, did it?

She gave a shake of her head, her raggedly layered hair dark and shining as it moved on her shoulders. 'I'm not sure which of us has imbibed the most champagne this evening, Max, but I do know I have no idea what you're talking about. So either you're talking gibberish, or I'm just too befuddled to understand you. Either way, I think it best if we terminate this conversation right now,' she added firmly, more than ever determined to follow through on her earlier decision to make her excuses and leave.

'This is my first drink of the evening.' Max held up his barely touched glass of champagne.

Implying she *was* the one who was 'too befuddled' to understand him. Well, he might just be right about that. It had been a long day—and an even longer evening.

She straightened determinedly. 'I wish I could say it's been a pleasure meeting you again, Mr Harding—'

'Oh, I think we're well enough acquainted now for you to call me Max,' he drawled mockingly. 'As you did a few minutes ago.'

They weren't acquainted at all—in fact, she knew less about this man than she had thought she did the first time she'd met him. 'If you say so.' She gave him an insincere smile, hoping they wouldn't meet again, so she wouldn't need to call him anything. 'I really do have to go now, Max,' she continued brightly. 'So, if you'll excuse me—? What are you doing?' she demanded indignantly as he reached out and grasped her arm when she would have turned and walked away.

It wasn't just that the physical contact was so unexpected—though it was!—but also that Max Harding didn't give the impression he was the touchy-feely type of man that always made her cringe. In fact, to date he had given the clear impression that his ice might be in danger of melting if he actually touched someone, and so he chose not to do it.

'Would you like me to give you a lift home?' came his also completely unexpected reply.

Abby frowned up at him, searching that enigmatic face for any hidden meaning behind his offer. But years of presenting an inscrutable expression to the world in general made that impossible.

'Why on earth would you want to do that?' Abby

couldn't keep the astonishment out of her voice. The last time the two of them had met he hadn't been able to get rid of her fast enough.

And yet he had been the one to approach her this evening—not once but twice, so perhaps...

'I haven't changed my mind about your show, Abby,' he assured her mockingly.

Which was exactly what she had been wondering! Were her thoughts so obvious to everyone? Or was it only this man who seemed to know what she was thinking?

That definitely wasn't a good idea, considering some of the thoughts she had been having about him. They swung erratically between being left breathless by his animal magnetism to actually wanting to hit him!

He was grinning when she glanced back at him—as if he had definitely been aware of *that* thought.

'You can't blame me for trying.' She shrugged dismissively, avoiding that knowing gaze.

'I never blame anyone for trying, Abby,' he retorted. 'But, to answer your earlier question, considering you know exactly where my apartment is, I thought it only fair that I should know where you live, too!'

'Fair' had nothing to do with it. Where this particular man was concerned she was a lot more comfortable with him *not* knowing where she lived!

'It's not far from here, actually,' she said evasively. 'In fact, I walked over this evening.'

He nodded. 'It's a pleasant spring evening. A walk sounds an excellent idea.'

Not with this man it didn't. And why was he being so persistent? He obviously thought her a lightweight in the world of television, and had made no effort to disguise the fact that he wasn't particularly enamoured of her as a woman, either—those remarks about her not being his type had stung! So why was he deliberately seeking out her company now?

His face, unfortunately, revealed none of his inner thoughts or emotions.

'There's really no need for you to accompany me,' she assured him lightly. 'This is one of the safer areas of London.'

'One of the more expensive ones, you mean,' Max drawled. 'I guess having your own show pays a lot more than being a weather girl?'

'I guess it does!' she snapped, blue eyes glittering angrily. He was so insulting!

In fact, she had been quite surprised at just how *much* more her change in status paid. Moving to a new apartment two months ago was only one of the changes it had made in her life. She had a sporty Jaguar in the underground car park of the apartment building, and the wardrobe allowance for her new show was almost more than she had earned in a year at her previous job.

Still, it was really none of his business.

'Do you ever say anything nice?'

'Sometimes—when I forget myself,' he said unrepentantly. 'Do you have somewhere else you have to go?'

'No—'

'Then let's go for that walk, shall we?' he announced briskly, giving her no further time to protest as he took a firm hold of her arm, quickly made their excuses to Dorothy, and pulled her along at his side as he made his way with assurance towards the door.

It had still been light outside when Abby had arrived a short time ago, but it was completely dark now. The high heels of her shoes echoed in the silence of this residential area of the city. In fact, it was almost as if they were the only two people around, with only the distant roar of the Friday evening traffic to confirm that they weren't.

Which wasn't nearly enough, as far as Abby was concerned. Max maintained his light but unshakeable hold on her arm as they walked along together, making her skin tingle with awareness. Maybe she was a 'normal red-blooded woman' after all!

Because awareness seemed to be coursing through her whole body. She was beginning to feel warm all over, her breathing shallow as she shot him a glance from beneath lowered dark lashes.

Dorothy was right. He really was gorgeous as hell. That overlong dark hair was crying out to have fingers running through it caressingly, and those sculptured lips, the bottom one fuller than the top, invited kisses. And as for the obvious power of the body beneath that formal evening suit—! Abby knew exactly how wide and muscled those shoulders were, clearly remembering the silky short hair on that powerful chest, the flatness of his tapered stomach, the force of his—

'You're very quiet— Careful!' Max steadied her as she stumbled slightly. 'Those strappy black sandals look great with your wonderful long legs,' he drawled, 'but they aren't very practical for walking anywhere!'

Max thought she had 'wonderful long legs'! It was amazing how the compliment gave her an inner glow.

Especially as until this moment she hadn't even thought he had noticed she *had* legs. The last—first—time they had met, she had been wearing denims. As for his remark about her being quiet—the more aware she became of him the more tongue-tied she felt. But she couldn't tell him that!

Instead she managed a casual shrug. 'You didn't give me the impression that you wanted to talk.'

'No?' He stood facing her now, his expression unreadable in the dim glow given off by the streetlights overhead. 'What did I give you the impression that I wanted to do instead?' His voice was huskily soft.

Abby swallowed hard, totally aware of how close he was standing, mere inches away from her—so close that the warmth of his breath stirred the feathery tendrils of hair on her forehead. She had no idea what Max wanted to do, while at the same time knowing exactly what she wanted him to do!

She wanted to have his lips against hers, to feel the lean strength of his arms about her as he moulded her body against his, to know the caress of his hands down her spine and against her sensitised breasts. And she wanted the same freedom to touch him intimately.

'Abby...?' he prompted softly at her continued silence. Breaking—thank goodness!—the emotional spell she had rapidly been falling under.

She gave herself a mental shake. This was Max Harding, for goodness' sake. A man who on first acquaintance she had decided was rude, arrogant and mocking—not to mention dangerous. She didn't even like him!

She still thought he was all of those things, but further acquaintance on her part had shown her he was also irresistibly attractive, sensually magnetic—and most definitely gorgeous. So much so that if he *had* kissed her a few moments ago, as she had so wanted him to, she knew she would have just melted into his arms, that the word 'no' would no longer have been part of her vocabulary.

But even acknowledging that to herself was enough to bring her to her senses with the suddenness of a bucket of water being thrown over her. This was Max Harding: cold, aloof and totally unobtainable!

She straightened, determinedly pulling her gaze away from the sensual kissability of those lips. 'Just walk me home and get this over with,' she instructed coolly, inwardly pleased at the normality of her tone— she had expected to sound like Minnie Mouse!

Max continued to look at her for several long seconds and then gave a curt nod of his head—whether of agreement to her statement or dismissal of it, Abby wasn't sure. 'Fine,' he rasped, no longer touching her as he strode forcefully ahead.

Leaving Abby to click-clack along behind him, in shoes that definitely weren't designed for it, in order to keep up with him. But she wasn't about to voice any complaint at the pace he had set. She just wanted to disappear into the privacy of her apartment now. Besides, she wouldn't give him the satisfaction!

Five minutes and probably a ruined pair of expensive shoes later, they reached the building that housed her apartment. 'Thank you for escorting me home,' she said with firm dismissal, and stood as if guarding the entrance to the building, having no intention of letting him get anywhere near her actual apartment.

'Very politely said!' Max's mouth twisted mockingly. 'Your mother and Dorothy obviously attended a good school.'

Abby gave him an impatient look, at the same time aware that there was something at the back of her mind that Max had said earlier, and it had been bothering her. 'What did you mean when you said I had relatives in high places?' She had thought it a strange remark at the time, but she had been slightly side-tracked after it and forgotten to pursue the subject.

Max tilted his head slightly as he looked down at her quizzically. 'You aren't trying to tell me that you don't know?' He sounded sceptical.

Her frown deepened. 'Don't know what?'

'About Paul Dillman's connection to Ajax Television—and consequently Dorothy's?' he drawled.

The obvious response to that was, What connection? But as she really didn't want to let this man know that she didn't have any idea what he was talking about, it was a question she had no intention of asking.

At least, not of Max.

CHAPTER FOUR

'PAUL recently became a major shareholder in Ajax Television,' Dorothy told her as she moved about her conservatory, watering her plants, glancing over only when Abby's silence lengthened. 'I thought I'd mentioned it to you?' the older woman prompted softly.

No, of course Dorothy hadn't mentioned it to her! If she had Abby might have questioned her sudden rise to fame a little more deeply. But she had genuinely thought it had happened as Pat Connelly had claimed—that Abby had done so well during her months of co-hosting the breakfast show that she was now being offered a show of her own.

Despite being awake most of the night thinking about this, she had waited until ten before calling to see Dorothy, aware that the party the evening before probably wouldn't have ended until late, and giving the other woman time to have a lie-in.

Abby hadn't been as lucky—unable to sleep at all after making her hurried goodbyes to Max and retreating to her apartment. Instead, she had paced up and down most of the night, wondering if what Max had claimed could possibly be true.

It obviously was!

Dorothy gave her a searching look. 'Abby? What difference does it make?'

'It makes a *lot* of difference,' Abby said sharply, feeling as if her whole world—well, her professional one, at least—was crashing down around her ears. First last night's disaster, and now this!

Dorothy put down her watering can, giving Abby her total attention now. 'I don't see why. Pat Connelly was the one to approach Ajax with the idea for the show. As I understood it, she had seen you on early-morning television and thought you had something more to give. Paul did become a shareholder a few months ago, Abby, but he's had very little to do with programme selection,' she added, when Abby still looked doubtful.

'Even if that's true—'

'It is,' the other woman assured her, with her customary briskness. 'Obviously when Paul was told of the idea of giving you your own chat show he was absolutely thrilled for you. But that's as far as his involvement went.' Dorothy's gaze sharpened suspiciously. 'Who has implied otherwise?'

Abby avoided meeting the older woman's gaze. 'It doesn't matter,' she said, deciding that perhaps it had been a mistake to question Dorothy about this—even if it had seemed the quickest way of getting an answer. 'I guess I'll just have to work twice as hard in an effort to prove those accusations of nepotism wrong, won't I?' she added with forced lightness.

'Who is "everyone"?' Dorothy looked most displeased. 'It isn't that awful Gary Holmes, is it?' she added disgustedly.

Abby's eyes widened. 'I didn't realise that you thought he was awful, too.'

Dorothy wrinkled her nose with distaste. 'I know he's wonderfully good-looking, darling, and that most women find him irresistible, but I'm well past the age where looks alone impress me. He made a pass at me once—which I thought totally out of line and Paul found highly amusing!' she added.

Abby gave a rueful smile at the image this evoked. 'No, for once this has nothing to do with Gary Holmes.'

'Who then? Not Max?' the older woman protested indignantly. 'Surely not…?' She seemed to be speaking to herself now rather than Abby. 'Despite what you said about him earlier in the evening, I noticed that the two of you seemed to be getting on well together last night. I was absolutely thrilled when you left together a short time later.'

'I can't imagine why,' Abby muttered with a dismissive shake of her head, glancing at her wristwatch. 'Is that really the time?' She feigned haste, although it was actually still only ten-thirty, and since it was a Saturday she had very little else to do but catch up on her laundry. But Max Harding, and yesterday evening were the last things she wanted to discuss right now—with Dorothy or anyone else.

'But we haven't even had coffee yet,' Dorothy protested. 'I was going to ring and have Dora make some.'

'I'll have to take a raincheck.' Abby smiled reassuringly—even though it was the last thing she felt like doing. 'I have to be somewhere else at eleven o'clock.' At home. With the door firmly locked. And the answering machine switched on to take any telephone calls.

Because at the moment she felt as if she needed a little time and space away from the rest of the world in order to lick her wounds in private.

Despite what Dorothy claimed to the contrary, she wasn't one hundred per cent convinced of Paul's non-involvement in choosing her to present Ajax Television's new Friday evening chat show.

'Just ignore it, Monty,' she advised her pet firmly as the doorbell rang for a second time in thirty seconds. 'Mum would have telephoned before coming, and I don't want to see anyone else.' She just wanted to continue sprawling on the sofa, Monty curled up on her chest, loudly purring his approval of this inactivity. 'You know, Monty, all I ever wanted—' She broke off as the doorbell rang a third time.

And kept ringing. And ringing. And ringing. Whoever her visitor was, he was keeping a finger continuously on the doorbell now.

Driving Abby insane!

'That's it!' She finally snapped after a good thirty seconds or so of the incessant nerve-jangling noise. She placed Monty gently on the cushioned sofa—attempting to do it any other way would probably have resulted in claw-flexing disapproval!—before standing up and pressing the intercom impatiently.

'Yes?' she snapped aggressively into the speaker, scowling. 'What is your problem?' She sounded as irritable as she felt, and was not in any sort of mood for visitors. Especially such a persistent one!

'Open the door, Abby,' a familiar voice drawled derisively.

Abby snatched her finger off the intercom as if it had burnt her. Max! What on earth was he doing here? Why—?

The doorbell began to ring again.

She pressed the intercom again. 'Will you stop doing that?'

'As soon as you open the door and let me in—yes,' he replied evenly.

She didn't want to open the door. Didn't want to see Max. Didn't want to speak to him. But the alternative, she realised as the bell began to ring again, was to be driven noisily insane by the sound of her own doorbell.

She pressed the door-release button, moving to shove open her apartment door too, before stomping back into the sitting room to throw herself back down onto the sofa—receiving a hiss and a scratch from Monty as she inadvertently sat down on him.

She picked up one of the cushions and hugged it to her defensively as she heard Max outside in the hallway, followed by the soft click of her apartment door closing as he let himself inside and came to stand in the lounge doorway. The still ruffled Monty refused to acknowledge her visitor by so much as a twitch of an eyebrow.

'Very nice,' Max murmured appreciatively as he moved forward into the room.

Abby was well aware that he couldn't be referring to her— the last time she had checked in the mirror she had looked less than her best. Her hair was in wild disorder from the light breeze blowing outside, and she'd made no effort to renew her lipgloss since her return from Dorothy's. He had to be commenting on her apartment.

It *was* very nice—the rooms spacious and grand, with a fantastic view over the Thames. But she was sure Max hadn't come here to discuss the comforts of her apartment. She didn't know what he *had* come here to discuss, but she was pretty sure it wasn't that!

'Max, what do you want?' she demanded rudely, keeping her gaze cool as she took in his appearance in those ragged denims and a black T-shirt.

God, he really was gorgeous, she acknowledged to herself. Her heart was beating erratically just at the sight of him.

'Coffee,' he replied briskly. 'Black. One sugar.' He dropped down into one of the comfortable armchairs.

Abby blinked dazedly. How did 'What do you want?' equate with 'Coffee. Black. One sugar'? And Monty was no help as a watch-cat either; he had beaten a hasty retreat into her bedroom at the first sound of Max's voice!

She frowned. 'I wasn't offering you anything to drink,' she told him impatiently.

'No?' He raised dark brows, his grey gaze moving slowly over her face before moving down to her slender curves in denims and a blue T-shirt. 'What were you offering me, then?'

Abby felt a betraying tingling down her spine as his husky, seductive tone washed over her, and knew that heat had coloured her cheeks.

Damn it, this man only had to look at her in a certain way, only had to talk to her in a certain way, and all she could think of was the nakedness of his body at that first meeting, her fingers aching to touch the silky dark hair on his chest.

She stood up restlessly, returning the cushion to the sofa. 'I was asking why you're here,' she explained succinctly.

Max looked up at her, gaze narrowed. 'You're looking tired today—didn't you sleep well?'

Abby glared at him. 'No, I didn't sleep well!' How

could she, after what he had told her about Paul's connection to Ajax Television?

He shrugged. 'The reviews were good in this morning's newspapers.'

Surprisingly, they had been—not all as sensationally headlined as Jenny Jones's rag, but very positive nonetheless. One more reputable newspaper had even commented that if the rest of *The Abby Freeman Show* proved to be as entertaining then she was a very welcome addition to the genre.

High praise indeed, but in Abby's mind none of that altered the fact that it hadn't been the show she had planned—or what she now knew of Paul's involvement with Ajax Television. If the formidable English press ever got hold of the fact that she had a personal connection to Dorothy Dillman then they would have a field-day!

'Or does your lack of sleep have anything to do with the fact that Dorothy telephoned me a short time ago and told me I have a big mouth?' Max added softly.

Abby's gaze swung instinctively to look at the mentioned feature. It was such a decisive-looking mouth— a mouth that in spite of herself she longed to kiss! Although at the moment it was set in a determined line as he waited for her answer.

'Did she?' Abby moistened her own lips with the tip of her tongue, her gaze not quite meeting his now.

'She did,' he confirmed with a pointed sigh. 'Something, as Dorothy happens to be one of my favourite people, I wasn't too pleased about. Even if—as I pointed out to her—I was just returning the compliment.' The steadiness of his gaze told her he was referring to the source who'd given her his address.

It was impossible to mistake his displeasure for anything else. The grey eyes were glittering, his earlier mocking humour gone without trace, his restless anger tangible in spite of the fact he still lounged back in the armchair.

'Dorothy is one of my favourite people, too,' she assured him quietly.

'I don't doubt it,' he rasped. 'But she hasn't just told *you* that you have a big mouth!'

No, and she couldn't imagine Dorothy having said that to Max, either. 'Dorothy is far too sweet to talk to anyone like that,' she argued.

Max shrugged. 'Ordinarily I would have said so too, but she told me to put it down to her age.'

Abby remembered that as the phrase her godmother had used the evening before, when discussing Jenny Jones, so perhaps Dorothy had said it after all. Abby's mother, Dorothy's best friend, had gone through the menopause several years ago, and she seemed to remember there had been something of a personality shift then, so maybe that was what Dorothy was referring to when she talked of her age being responsible for her uncharacteristic outspokenness.

'Well, I'm sorry if it was anything I said that caused Dorothy to talk to you in that way.' Abby sighed. 'But, after what you said last night, I needed some answers to some questions, and in the circumstances Dorothy seemed the obvious choice to give them to me.' Even if, as far as Abby was concerned, those answers had been less than satisfactory.

'How about I take you out and we discuss this further over lunch?'

Abby stared at Max now, too stunned by the suggestion to hide her surprise. 'You're inviting me out to lunch?' She looked at him suspiciously.

His mouth twitched as he easily read her disbelief. 'That would seem to be what I just did, yes,' he confirmed mockingly.

Her stare turned to a frown. Why on earth would Max Harding, of all people, be inviting her out to lunch? It was—

'You think too much, Abby,' he told her irritably, and he stood up. 'Grab a jacket and let's go.'

Did she want to go out to lunch with Max Harding? The answer to that was a definite yes!

And it had absolutely nothing to do with continuing her efforts to persuade him to appear on her show, on the basis that any dialogue between them was better than none, and everything to do with the fluttering sensation in her chest and her complete physical awareness of him.

He took some car keys out of the pocket of his ragged denims. 'Yes or no, Abby?'

A part of her so badly wanted to say no—if only to see the look on his face when she did. But the rest of her wanted to say yes—even if she did know it was a mistake to be attracted to this man.

'I'll take your silence as a no,' he rasped impatiently as he turned to leave.

'Yes!' Abby burst out forcefully.

Max came to a halt, slowly turning to face her, his expression unreadable. 'Yes, I can take that as a no? Or, yes, you'll have lunch with me?' His offhand tone implied he was no longer bothered either way.

Which he probably wasn't, Abby accepted ruefully. He had made the gesture—for whatever reason—and the rest was up to her. It was a sure fact that if she said no now he would never repeat the invitation.

'Yes, I'll come to lunch.' She plucked her jacket from the back of the chair, where she had thrown it earlier, deftly slipping her arms into the sleeves. 'After all, a free lunch is a free lunch!' she added with casual dismissal. No need to look too eager!

Max eyed her mockingly. 'Didn't you know, Abby? There's no such thing as a free lunch.'

Maybe there wasn't, but she couldn't for the life of her imagine what price he might consider extracting for buying her lunch; after all, he had told her on several occasions that she wasn't his type. And even if she was, that price might be a little high!

He sighed, indicating his impatience with her delay. 'Would you just get your act in gear? I get tetchy when I'm hungry,' he added ruefully.

Abby slung the strap of her bag over her shoulder. 'How can you tell?' she taunted as she passed him on her way to the door.

'Oh, ha-ha,' he muttered. 'You'll see—I'll be a veritable pussycat once I've eaten.'

A lion or a tiger, maybe. Or at least one of the man—woman?—eating kind!

But, talking of cats…

'Just a minute.' She beat a hasty retreat back into the apartment, going through to the kitchen to check that Monty had enough water while she was out.

When she returned to the lounge she discovered that Monty had left his hiding place and was now graciously allowing Max to get down on his haunches and stroke his silky white fur.

'My cat Monty.' She introduced him wryly. Her *trai-*

torous cat Monty. Really, couldn't Monty recognise an enemy when he saw one?

Max looked up at her. 'This isn't just a cat, Abby, he's a Persian. Rather a magnificent example of his breed, too,' he added admiringly.

'Oh, don't you start!' She raised her eyes heavenwards. 'Monty already has an elevated enough opinion of himself as it is.'

'Quite right too,' Max straightened. 'Are you finally ready to go?'

'Well, I could always do a little dusting, and the bedroom probably needs tidying… Yes, I'm ready to go now!' she taunted lightly, and he shot her a scathing look.

She was even more pleased she had accepted his invitation when she realised he was driving to her favourite restaurant. She loved Italian food, and Luigi's served some of the finest in London. The busy restaurant also had the advantage of being close to the studio where she now worked. Not that it mattered today; she wasn't going back in to work until Monday.

'I asked Dorothy where you like to eat,' Max told her as he saw her pleased expression. Which meant he had intended inviting her out to lunch all the time…

Interesting.

Although the fact that Dorothy knew Max meant to invite her out to lunch probably meant that her mother now knew about it too.

The two women—Dorothy and Abby's mother Elizabeth—spoke on the telephone at least a couple of times a week, and Abby was sure that Dorothy would consider Abby being invited out to lunch by Max Harding as more than enough reason for one of those lengthy calls. Max probably had no idea, but, knowing the two women as well as she did, Abby had no doubt that by the time the telephone conversation came to an end Dorothy and Elizabeth would have chosen the colour of the bridesmaids' dresses and decided on names for their children.

'What's so funny?' Max prompted after parking the silver Mercedes and coming round to open her door for her.

She gave a dismissive shake of her head. 'You had to be there!'

His mouth twisted derisively. 'Maybe I would have been if I'd known it was going to be so much fun!'

No, he wouldn't. One thing she could say with absolute certainty about Max Harding—without any fear of contradiction on his part—was that he certainly wasn't the type of man you took home to meet your mother!

As far as Abby was aware, apart from that very early marriage, at thirty-nine years old he had never been involved in a relationship that even approached that level of seriousness.

She wondered why that was. There was no doubting his good looks, or his sensual attraction, and he was certainly wealthy enough, so Abby was sure that his reluctance about commitment couldn't have come from the females he'd dated. Maybe—

'What are you thinking about now?' Max enquired, his hand lightly on her elbow as they crossed the car park to the restaurant.

Abby gave him a look from beneath lowered lashes. 'The truth?'

'I find that preferable.'

She drew in a deep breath. 'I was wondering if perhaps you had homosexual tendencies.'

'You were wondering—!' Max broke off incredulously. 'By all means be blunt, why don't you?' He gave a dazed shake of his head.

'Well, you did ask.'

'I know I did. And the answer is no. A definite no,' he added impatiently.

Abby gave an unconcerned shrug. 'It was just a thought.'

Max swung open the restaurant door for her to enter. 'Well, in future I suggest you keep those sort of thoughts to yourself!'

'You asked,' she protested. 'Besides, you said I wasn't your type, so I—'

'Jumped to a conclusion a dozen steps ahead rather than one!' He shook his head. 'And I wasn't referring to the whole of the female sex, anyway.'

'Just me?'

He gave her a considering look, that sweeping gaze taking in the whole of her appearance from her silky dark hair to her booted feet. 'I think it might be best if I were to reserve judgement on my previous statement,' he finally answered huskily.

'You sound like a lawyer,' Abby mocked.

'I shall be "taking the fifth" in a moment,' he assured her sardonically.

She shook her head. 'I don't think that applies over here.'

'Then maybe it should,' Max said with feeling.

Exactly what had he meant by that remark? Abby wondered with a fluttering sensation in her chest. Could he—?

'Abby!' Luigi himself was acting as *maître d'* today, smiling his pleasure as he moved to kiss her on both cheeks. 'Such an honour to have you with us today,' he beamed. 'For obvious reasons I couldn't see your show myself last night.' He looked pointedly around the crowded restaurant, which was even more frenetic in the evenings. 'But my wife tells me it was very romantic.' He raised his eyebrows suggestively.

Abby laughed, making no comment on the show herself; as far as she was concerned the jury was still out on whether or not it had actually been a success. 'Luigi, this is Max Harding.' She changed the subject by introducing the two men.

'But of course.' Luigi clearly recognized him. 'It is a pleasure to meet you, Mr Harding.'

'Max, please,' he responded smoothly. 'I telephoned earlier and booked a table,' he told the corpulent Italian.

'I had no idea Abby was to be your dining companion.' The restaurant owner smiled, removing a 'Reserved' sign from a table in the middle of the room and taking them to a window table instead.

'You eat here quite often, I gather?' Max murmured dryly, obviously having noticed the move.

'Often enough,' she agreed, nodding to several people in the restaurant whom she knew—quite a lot of them from the studio down the street.

Max had been so sure that he could persuade her to have lunch with him today that he had booked a table? That sort of confidence, and the fact that she was here and proving it justified, made her feel more than a little annoyed. Was she that easy to read? Or just that easy?

'Dorothy warned me I'd need to book a table if we weren't to be disappointed when we got here,' Max put in quietly, perhaps noticing her rapidly rising indignation.

Seated opposite him, totally aware of him and anticipating one of Luigi's delicious pasta dishes for lunch rather than the crackers and cheese she had intended having at home, Abby decided she couldn't be bothered to argue.

'A glass of your house red, please,' she told Luigi in answer to his question concerning drinks. 'It's very good,' she assured Max as he looked at her enquiringly.

'Make that two glasses of house red—thanks,' he told the other man, before turning his attention back to Abby. 'So how does it feel to be a celebrity?'

She grimaced, fiddling with the small vase of fresh flowers in the middle of the table. 'If I ever become one I'll be sure to let you know!'

Max reached out and put one of his much larger hands over both of hers. 'Take a look around you, Abby,' he advised softly.

She did, her eyes widening as she saw that a lot of the other diners were now sending surreptitious glances in their direction. One or two of those people were actually smiling at her approvingly.

She gave a rueful shrug as she turned back to Max. 'They're probably all wondering who the woman is having lunch with Max Harding!'

He gave a shake of his head. 'I'm yesterday's news, Abby. It's you they're looking at,' he assured her.

Another slightly self-conscious look around the room confirmed that he was right—that she *was* the one people were nodding and smiling at.

She had come in for her fair share of recognition from being on breakfast television for over a year, but nothing like this. Then she had usually been recognised and stopped in the supermarket buying her week's supply of chocolate—or, even worse, in the chemist as she was buying essential but embarrassing female toiletries.

But most of that recognition had been from middle-aged or elderly females; the wave of awareness she could feel in the restaurant now was coming from both males and females—of all ages. Recognition and smiling approval, she realized. Most of those friendly gazes seemed to be smiling indulgently at the hold Max still had on her hands.

She hastily removed her hands from his. 'They'll have the two of us married to each other by tomorrow morning!' she explained with fiery red cheeks.

'Possibly,' Max acknowledged lightly, sitting back with apparent unconcern. 'Need any more confirmation that your show was a success?'

'Lots!' She grimaced. 'Especially as the whole thing seems to be a case of "not what I know but who I know" getting me the job in the first place,' she recalled heavily.

It might also help to explain Gary Holmes's obvious contempt for her from the start—he had known of her relationship to Paul Dillman's wife. Although Max certainly hadn't been aware of that connection until she had told him… Oh, well, perhaps Gary Holmes was just rude and cutting to any young upstart he considered had been foisted on him. Whatever—he certainly didn't like her.

'Well, well, well, Abby. Out for a celebration lunch? Or is it one of commiseration?' The last word dripped with scorn.

Perhaps it was thinking about him, or maybe he was just becoming her nemesis, but Abby could only look up in open-mouthed dismay as Gary Holmes himself materialised beside their table. In fact, she was so surprised she couldn't even speak.

In the event, it was Max who answered the other man. 'A celebration, of course, Gary,' he assured him challengingly as he stood up.

To say Gary looked stunned at the identity of her dining companion was putting it mildly. The older man's face was suffused with heated colour. What followed was the draining of all that colour, leaving him white and drawn.

Max, in contrast, looked arrogantly assured at he stared down at the other, shorter and more slenderly built man.

Gary swallowed convulsively as he tried to return that hard gaze. 'Max,' he muttered unnecessarily.

Max gave a humourless smile, his eyes glittering icily. 'At least neither of us is hypocritical enough to say it's good to see you again.'

Because it obviously wasn't, Abby saw.

The one and only time Gary Holmes's name had come up in conversation between herself and Max had been that first day, when Abby had managed to get herself admitted into Max's apartment. She remembered that Max had gone very quiet afterwards, brushing off her question and changing the subject when she had asked him for an explanation. But now, seeing the two men together, she knew her instinct that day had been correct. These two men heartily disliked each other.

She wondered why.

But Gary was recovering rapidly now, his initial shock fading to be replaced by his usual sneering smile as he turned back to look at Abby. 'Can I take it from the two of you being here together that you have succeeded in persuading Max to come on your show after all?' he taunted.

'You can take it any way you like, Gary,' Max answered harshly. 'Now, if you wouldn't mind? You've interrupted our meal for quite long enough.' He gave the other man a pointedly dismissive look.

'Not at all.' Gary was obviously fully recovered now. 'I'll look forward to working with you again,' he added challengingly, before shooting Abby once last dismissive glance and swaggering his way out of the restaurant.

Abby looked curiously up at Max as he still stood beside the table.

Again. Gary had said he looked forward to working with Max *again.*

When had the two men worked together in the past? Whenever it was, it clearly hadn't been a friendly relationship!

She moistened dry lips. 'Max—'

'Don't ask!' he rasped, his expression harsh and remote as he resumed his seat.

But she wanted to know—needed to know before she worked with Gary again. She was sure that the other man wouldn't let this chance meeting pass without further comment. Which, in her ignorance, she would have no chance of combating.

But Max's frostily closed expression certainly didn't invite further questions on the subject!

In fact, Gary's uninvited appearance had put a complete dampener on their meal together. Neither of them—to Luigi's obvious disgust—did more than pick at the homemade pasta, and both of them refused dessert or coffee.

Max asked tersely for the bill before driving her home in stony silence.

All of which brought Abby to the decision that the

first thing she would do on Monday morning was set about finding out the history of the obvious antagonism between Max Harding and Gary Holmes.

She had a feeling it was a history worth knowing.

CHAPTER FIVE

'I'M SORRY.'

Abby, half in the car, half out on the pavement, paused to turn and look at Max. 'Sorry for what?'

After starting out so promisingly, she had just suffered through the most awful lunch of her life; there had better only be one thing he was sorry for!

His expression darkened. 'Damn it!' His hands tightened briefly on the steering wheel before he turned to push the car door open beside him and stepped forcefully onto the road—instantly having to hold up a hand of apology to the driver of an oncoming car, who had to veer further out into the road to avoid hitting him. Max strode round the car to stand on the pavement next to the watching Abby. 'I'm sorry I was such a lousy lunch companion,' he muttered.

Not the most gracious apology she had ever received, but for all that Abby could see that it was sincere. Although his grim expression didn't exactly encourage questions as to *why* he had been so angry and bad-tempered throughout their meal. She knew the who, of course, just not the why...

But now probably wasn't the time to pursue the subject. 'I didn't notice,' she came back lightly, eyes glowing with mischief as she met his gaze.

'Yeah, right,' he drawled self-mockingly, his dark mood seeming to ease somewhat.

'Would you like to come up for the coffee we both refused at Luigi's?'

Max gave her a look. 'The last woman to invite me in for coffee had something else in mind.'

'I'm only offering coffee,' she assured him dryly.

At least, she thought she was…

Because, despite—or because of!—his lack of conversation during lunch, Abby's awareness of him had only grown. To the point where she was acutely aware of every move he made, of the dark hair visible above his T-shirt, of the way that fitted T-shirt emphasised the powerful width of his shoulders and chest, of the hard sensuality of his face, of the way his hair fell endearingly across his forehead…

She hoped she was only inviting him in for coffee…

His sensuality was something she was too aware of. His aura of totally masculine power touched and inflamed something deep inside her—something that had been totally unknown to her until today. Total physical awareness. And it completely took her breath away. Her body felt incredibly warm, her legs and arms lethargic.

She hoped Max wasn't aware of it, too!

He didn't appear to be as he locked the car before taking a light hold on her arm. 'Remind me to have a word with you later about the fragility of a man's ego,' he told her dryly as she let them both into the apartment building.

Some men's egos, perhaps, Abby thought as they went up together in the lift. The research she had already done on *this* man told her that just because he had never remarried it didn't mean there had been a shortage of women in his life—she had been being deliberately provocative earlier, when she'd questioned his sexual preference! And he was usually the one to bring an end—usually an abrupt end—to his relationships.

Which warned her that she would be a fool to follow up her own obvious attraction to him—if she needed any warning...

Research was one thing, but the man himself was a puzzle within an enigma. And Abby had a distinct feeling he preferred it like that. An only child of wealthy parents, who had lived mainly on the island of Majorca for the last ten years, with no other emotional ties, Max was pretty much a law unto himself.

And everything about him shouted that he intended remaining that way.

Not that Abby was interested in a serious relationship with anyone, either. Her last relationship, of six months' duration, had ended several months ago, and she was in no hurry to repeat the experience of someone wanting to know what she was doing and what she was thinking twenty-four hours a day! Besides, Monty hadn't liked Andrew at all—arching his back and hissing whenever he'd seen him.

But he liked Max, a little voice whispered inside her head.

Something that was reaffirmed when Abby came back from the kitchen carrying two mugs of steaming hot coffee and found Monty sitting majestically on Max's knee, his whole body one big purr.

'What can I say? He likes me!' Max laughed huskily as he saw her disgusted look.

Abby put one of the mugs down on the table in

front of him. 'Enough to have restored that fragile male ego?' she taunted as she sat down in the chair opposite.

'Well, I wouldn't go that far.' He shrugged, his expression sobering. 'I really am sorry about lunch. I invited you out, and then behaved like a bad-tempered idiot throughout. Gary Holmes will do that to me every time!' he added harshly.

Abby eyed him over the top of her coffee mug. 'I know why I don't like him, but what did he ever do to you?'

Max's expression was grim, his eyes glacial. 'I took you out to lunch because I thought we needed to talk, not so that I could answer questions—'

'But we didn't talk, Max,' Abby cut in pointedly, deciding to ignore his deliberate challenge, though she was aware that he was reverting back to that coldly arrogant man of their first meeting, those barriers coming down like the steel of prison bars.

'No, we didn't,' he acknowledged harshly, looking at her with piercing grey eyes. 'Because Holmes's remarks made me realise that I had stupidly allowed myself to become sidetracked from the fact that you're still just another reporter looking for an angle. Worse—you're a chat-show host looking for an angle.' He put Monty to one side before standing up.

That last remark hurt—on two fronts. Personally, because she liked this man far more than was good for her. And professionally, because the intensifying attraction she felt towards this man had made her forget all about her job. The truth was, she found Max so physically mesmerising that she hadn't even thought about her show the whole time they had been together—or the fact that she still wanted him as her final guest.

It was this latter realisation that brought her to her feet, too, eyes sparkling with resentment now. 'You are being extremely unfair,' she snapped. 'I never so much as— What do you mean, you "allowed" yourself to become sidetracked?' she demanded with a frown.

Max gave a humourless smile. '*Stupidly* allowed myself to become sidetracked,' he corrected harshly, that icy grey gaze unfathomable as it swept over her with calculation.

Abby withstood his cold look with a challenging lift of her chin, knowing from the contemptuous curl of those sculptured lips that whatever he was looking at certainly wasn't the same reflection *she* saw when she looked in the mirror every morning.

And the tension was unbearable. The very air seemed to crackle between them as their gazes remained locked in silent battle.

Abby was determined—childishly?—not to be the first to break that gaze. No, not childishly; there was nothing in the least child-like about the way she was looking at Max. Or the way he was looking at her. In fact, his gaze had become altogether adult in its appraisal now, those grey eyes seeming to frown disapprovingly even as his gaze shifted to her mouth.

She couldn't help what happened next: it was pure instinct that made her run her tongue self-consciously over the lips he was frowning at so darkly. A move that only seemed to make his expression become grimmer than ever.

She sighed. 'Look, Max, I don't know—'

'Oh, you know, Abby,' he ground out, even as he stepped towards her. 'You really can't be that naïve!' he added scornfully.

But she was! In fact she had no idea what he was talking about—what she had done…

Every coherent thought left her head as Max reached out to grasp her arms and pull her into the hardness of his body, lowering his head as his lips claimed hers.

She did know, after all. *This* was what Max was talking about. *This* was what had sidetracked him earlier— he was as aware of her as she was of him.

It was a punishing kiss. Max completely skipped the tentative, the gentle exploration, going straight to heated passion, his mouth possessing hers with a fierceness Abby more than returned. Her arms slid up his chest as she pushed the jacket from his shoulders and threw it over onto the sofa, and his arms were like steel bands as he moulded her soft curves against the powerful hardness of his, at the same time making her fully aware of his arousal.

She was so hot, so aware, every nerve, every sense heightened as she kissed him back with all the pent-up emotion of the last couple of hours. This was what she wanted, what she had longed for since the moment she had first looked at Max Harding.

He felt so good, his shoulders so wide and muscled. He smelt so good, a light cologne only adding to the musky smell that tantalised her senses as much as the lips exploring hers with such thoroughness. His hands were now seeking the pleasure spots of her body, palms running firmly down her spine before moving forward to cup her breasts, the soft pads of his thumbs moving rhythmically against the hardened tips.

Abby gasped with pleasure, groaning low in her throat as Max's tongue sought and found hers, before exploring the moist hollows of her mouth, touching nerve-endings she hadn't known existed, taking her to heights she had never known. She was aware only of Max, of the touch of his hands, his lips, his tongue. Every particle of her, it seemed, was consumed by a need that was rapidly growing out of control inside her. She—

She suddenly found herself thrust away from him at arm's length, blinking up at him dazedly, knowing by the flush above the hard cheekbones that he had been as aroused as she was, and with no idea what had caused him to bring a halt to their lovemaking. It certainly hadn't been because of a lack of response on her part, she acknowledged with a certain amount of self-derision, her cheeks becoming heated with the awareness of the depths of her arousal.

She shook her head. 'Max, what—?'

'You have a visitor,' he rasped, eyes glittering as his hands briefly tightened on her arms before he released her with a suddenness that made her stumble slightly. At the same time the doorbell buzzed—for the second time?

If someone had buzzed up already then Abby hadn't been aware of it—completely lost in her desire for Max, in the way he had kissed and tantalised her. But Max obviously hadn't been as mindlessly aroused as her.

'Shouldn't you answer that?' he bit out abruptly, thrusting his hands into his pockets, his expression darkly brooding as he looked at her.

Should she? Did she really want to see anyone just now? Besides, who could it be? Her parents lived in the country, she had seen Dorothy only this morning, and at the moment, with the sexual tension still tangible between herself and Max, she didn't want to see anyone else.

She shook her head. 'I'm not expecting anyone.' Her

gaze locked on Max as she searched for signs of his arousal. And found none.

'No?' He quirked dark, sceptical brows as the buzzer sounded—more persistently this time.

Abby gave a pained frown. They needed to talk, not to be interrupted by a third party. Any third party. The kiss just now had proved that Max was as attracted to her as she was to him. That was why he had become 'sidetracked', as he'd put it, and they needed—

'Just now was a mistake, Abby,' Max told her harshly as he seemed to read her thoughts. 'One not to be repeated!'

'But—'

'Get the damned door!' he grated as the buzzer sounded again. 'I'm leaving, anyway,' he added, sounding disgusted, as he shrugged back into his jacket.

She could feel the heat of tears in her eyes at this total rejection of her, of what they had just shared. But she knew she hadn't imagined his response to her; she wasn't *that* inexperienced!

But in the face of his denial, and the return of the ice-man from their first meeting, she knew she would be a fool to pursue it, that she would be only leaving herself wide open to further humiliation. Worse, Max was more than capable of verbally annihilating her if she pushed him any further on the subject.

With one last lingering glance at the rigidity of his uncompromising back she walked dejectedly over to the door to press the intercom. 'Yes?' she said dispiritedly, not in the mood to speak to anyone right now. Except Max. And he didn't want to speak to her.

Maybe, if they hadn't been interrupted like this

maybe they would have ended up in bed together! After which Max would still have left…

'Not interrupting anything, am I, Abby?'

She stiffened, her eyes widening incredulously as she recognised Gary Holmes's insolent tone. She turned quickly to look at Max, knowing by the iciness of his gaze, the sudden tension of his body, that he had recognised the other man's voice too.

What was Gary doing here? He had never been to her apartment before—had never been invited! Well, he hadn't been invited this time either, but he was still here. And it couldn't have happened at a worse time!

What was Max thinking about the other man turning up here?

Hard to tell from that arrogantly closed expression. Certainly nothing good, anyway.

'Abby?' Gary Holmes prompted irritably at her continued silence.

Max's mouth twisted contemptuously. 'He seems to be getting impatient. I should let him in if I were you.'

Well, he wasn't her. And as far as she was concerned Gary Holmes had no right being here. She didn't like him, and certainly didn't want to invite him into her home. He might be the director of her show, but that gave him no right to invade her personal life.

She gave Max one last resentful glare before turning away to speak into the intercom. 'What do you want, Gary?'

He gave an audible chuckle. 'Now, that's a leading question!'

Not as far as he was concerned, it wasn't! Not as far as Max was concerned either, if the scornful way he was looking at her was anything to go by.

She gave an impatient sigh. 'I'm not in the mood for your mind games right now, Gary, so just say what you have to say and then go.'

'That isn't very friendly of you, Abby,' Gary drawled unconcernedly. 'I have a few things I need to discuss with you.'

'We'll talk on Monday—'

'I want to talk to you now, not Monday,' he cut in cheerfully. 'Look, why don't I walk up, instead of taking the lift, and give the two of you time to put some clothes on—'

'How dare you?' Abby gasped, shooting Max a panicked glance.

Gary knew that Max was up here with her, knew they had been making love—even if he had got their state of dress slightly wrong. Although if he had arrived ten minutes or so later, he might not have done…

'Oh, for God's sake, stop acting like some outraged virgin and open the door, Abby!' Gary rasped.

She didn't resist as Max appeared at her side, putting her firmly out of the way before pressing the intercom button. 'I have a better idea, Gary,' he bit out coldly. 'Abby will leave the door locked, and you can go and—'

'Really, Max,' Gary interrupted tauntingly. 'I'm sure you shouldn't be using language like that in front of a lady. And Abby is so very *much* a lady, isn't she?' he continued tauntingly. 'Wealthy parents, private schooling, not having to work her way through university, with the sort of looks and body all that money can buy. Class, with a capital C, that's our Abby—'

'I am not your Abby, damn it!' she was stung into shouting.

'No?' Gary came back mildly. 'Okay, if that's the

way you want to play it. I guess I'll speak to you later, after all. Bye, Max,' he added mockingly.

What was Gary doing? What was he implying? There was only the sound of static on the intercom now.

One glance at Max's icily contemptuous expression and she knew exactly what Gary had been trying to do. Surely Max couldn't really think—couldn't honestly believe—?

But as Max turned away, his expression now more coldly remote than ever, Abby could see that was exactly what he believed.

She drew in a shaky breath, realising as she did so that she was actually trembling. Not surprisingly. First that passionate explosion between herself and Max, quickly followed by this totally unwanted visit from Gary Holmes!

The latter she would have to deal with later—and deal with it she would! The former—well, Max already looked in the process of leaving…

'Max, you can't believe—'

'It doesn't matter what I believe, Abby.'

'But it does,' she protested emotionally. 'I have no idea what—what all that was about.' She gestured in the direction of the intercom. 'I'll have to talk to Gary about that on Monday,' she added determinedly. 'But you can't allow Gary Holmes's warped sense of humour to affect us—'

'Us?' Max repeated tauntingly, smiling with grim humour as he shook his head. 'A few kisses and a little light groping do not make an "us", Abby,' he dismissed.

A few kisses and—! Abby felt her cheeks suffuse with humiliated colour. First Gary, and now this—it was just too much!

She drew herself up to her full height of five feet four

inches, her chin raised challengingly. 'I think you had better leave—'

'Before I say something I'll regret?' Max finished scornfully, his hooded gaze unreadable. 'In the circumstances, do you really think that's possible?'

Probably not, she thought, swallowing her inward misery. If he didn't go soon—very soon—she was very much afraid she might just break down and cry—and in the circumstances that was the last thing she wanted to do in front of Max.

She had no idea what game Gary was playing, or why he should have guessed that Max was up here with her. When Gary had seen the two of them together at the bistro they hadn't so much as kissed each other yet, had surely given off no air of intimacy. Maybe his game was really just with Max—there had certainly been enough animosity between the two men earlier. If that were the case, then she didn't care for being caught in the middle of their obviously long-standing dislike of each other.

Besides, Max obviously couldn't wait to get away from here. From her. And she needed him to go, too, if only so that she could think clearly enough to try and make some sense of what had just happened between the two of them. If there was any sense to be made of it…

She gave a confident shake of her head. 'You aren't interested in what I think, Max.'

'You're right,' he shot back sharply. 'I'm not.' His mouth twisted derisively. 'Good luck with the show next week.'

He didn't really mean that either, Abby knew, as he turned abruptly on his heel, her apartment door slamming forcefully behind him seconds later.

Which was the signal for the tears she had so determinedly held in check to fall hotly down her cheeks.

She had never felt so humiliated in all her life—and, added to that, she didn't know which man she was the most angry with. Max or Gary.

Ten minutes later, her tears all cried out, the comforting Monty purring as he lay curled up on her lap, she had decided that on reflection Gary was the one who most deserved her wrath.

And he was going to get it!

'You have to understand, darling,' Dorothy soothed patiently. 'As Paul has just told you, what you've asked for simply can't be done.'

'Why can't it?' Abby snapped, eyes flashing deeply blue. 'I'm the presenter of the show; Gary is the director. And I'm no longer happy for him to direct me across a road!'

The last twenty-four hours had done nothing to lessen Abby's anger. In fact she had barely slept the night before, for thinking about what had happened with Max and Gary. The weekend with her parents had been as lovely as usual, their company calming, but it hadn't deterred her from her purpose in the slightest; she no longer wanted to work with Gary Holmes.

The first thing she had done after travelling back into London was call and see Paul and Dorothy, with the sole intent of asking Paul to support the demand she planned to make on Monday to have Gary removed as her director. A request he had just turned down.

Not that she had told Paul all the personal reasons why she no longer felt she could work with Gary—

only that personal dislike on both sides, meant that even a professional relationship between them couldn't work.

Paul had listened, nodding his head in all the right places, murmuring understandingly about 'professional differences', but finally had informed her, before leaving the two women alone together, that he didn't have the necessary reasons to support removing the highly experienced Gary from his position.

Dorothy smiled at her now. 'He has a binding contract, Abby—'

'So do I.' She paced the room restlessly, having already refused Dorothy's request for her to sit down. 'And nowhere in that contract does it say I have to work with a man so obnoxious you've told me you won't have him in your home!' She was breathing hard in her agitation.

'I somehow doubt there's anything in that contract that says you *don't* have to either,' her godmother said ruefully, at the same time giving her a considering look. 'What's happened since yesterday to make you so vehemently opposed to him? He hasn't been sexually harassing you, too, has he?' Dorothy looked suddenly alarmed. 'Because I'm sure under those circumstances Paul would act.'

Abby gave her a humourless smile. 'Sorry to disappoint you, Aunt Dorothy, but no sexual harassment to report.'

'I'm not in the least disappointed.' The older woman gave her a reproving look. 'Just trying to understand this sudden aversion to the man. I thought you had spent the rest of the weekend with Elizabeth and Jeremy?'

She had, having left for her parents' house almost immediately after Max left—as soon as her tears had dried and she'd realised she couldn't just simply sit around in her apartment all weekend brooding. She'd had to get out of there, away from the memories of being in Max's arms and the awful scene that had followed.

And so she had bundled Monty into his travelling basket—one where he could see and be seen, of course; Monty only tolerated those train journeys to her parents' on the understanding that he would be duly admired by fellow travellers on the journey, with the added knowledge that he would get to roam freely around the big, rambling vicarage that was the family home.

Wouldn't Max have fun with that little piece of information? She was the daughter of a vicar—and an ex-actress...

It had all the makings of one of those awful jokes, but Abby knew that her parents' marriage was far from a joke. The unlikely pair had been happily married for the last thirty years, and as their only child she had always been surrounded by their love and cosseting.

Which was exactly what she had needed these last twenty-four hours, away from London and all its complications.

Thoughts of Max she had put completely from her mind—they were just too complicated for her to deal with!—giving her time and distance to decide what she had to do about Gary Holmes. Unfortunately, Paul didn't seem to be willing to help her with the decision she had made.

'I did,' she answered Dorothy now. 'But Gary Holmes came to my apartment before I left for Hampshire. No, not for anything like that!' she snapped as Dorothy raised interested brows. 'He's so smug. So superior. As if he knows something that I don't. Oh, I'm sure that he knows a lot of things that I don't,' she went on ruefully as the older woman gave her a teasing look, 'and I'm well aware of what an experienced director he is, that he's been in the business almost twenty years—but, Dorothy, don't you find it strange that no men, and only silly women, seem to actually like the man?'

The other woman shrugged. 'I don't suppose it's essential to being brilliant at his job.'

'No, but—Dorothy, he *wanted* my show to be a disaster on Friday night!'

'Now, that *is* silly, darling,' her godmother reasoned. 'As the director, there could be absolutely no personal benefit to him if that had happened.'

Abby knew that—didn't understand the reasoning herself. She only knew that Gary had seemed disappointed the show hadn't failed on Friday night, that he had *wanted* her to fall flat on her face. In fact, she wouldn't be surprised if he hadn't known of the Brad/Natalie reconciliation! His taunt in the bistro yesterday, about her lunch being a celebration or a commiseration, had seemed to confirm his malevolence. Only the fact that Max had jumped to her defence, and Gary had obviously been not at all pleased to see him there, seemed to have stopped Gary from saying something even more scathing.

She had thought all this through over the weekend and knew that she was right—she just had no idea why.

And, without any reason, she realised that her request to Paul must have sounded slightly ridiculous.

'You're right, Dorothy,' she accepted with a sigh. 'No personal benefit at all.'

Except… As a relative newcomer, if her show should fail she would simply fade away into obscurity. As a seasoned director, and a brilliant one at that—Abby would allow him that!—Gary Holmes would simply move on to directing something else, with no detriment to his career at all.

But was that enough reason for what she suspected...?

Dorothy moved with her as Abby walked to the door. 'Don't be angry with Paul, Abby,' she pleaded. 'I'm sure that if you can come up with something concrete against the man, Paul would be only too happy to help. It's just that, as things stand, if he were to do anything now Ajax Television is likely to be slapped with an unfair dismissal charge. I suppose they could always ask him to resign and see what— No, I wouldn't advise that, either.' She winced. 'The man is just horrible enough to enjoy the fact that you obviously don't like working with him.'

Abby knew her godmother was right. She just wished that she wasn't. She also wished she had some answer to the dilemma herself.

But she didn't.

The telephone was ringing as she let herself into her apartment half an hour later, pausing briefly to open Monty's basket and let him out before hurrying to answer it.

The dial tone buzzed in her ear as she held up the receiver. And yet the ringing sound continued.

Because it wasn't *her* telephone ringing, she realised after a couple of confused seconds.

She put the receiver slowly back on its cradle, frowning her confusion as she looked around the sitting room for the source of the ringing. Her search becoming physical as the noise persisted, seeming to become more urgent by the second as she lifted cushions and newspapers in an effort to locate it.

A mobile phone! Lying half under her sofa, its ringing becoming louder as Abby brought it out fully.

Yes, it was a mobile—but whose? Because it certainly wasn't hers. That was switched off, in her shoulder bag. And she had vacuumed the sitting room yesterday morning; she was sure it hadn't been there then. Only Max had been in her apartment since that time...

She stared down at the silver-coloured mobile with rapidly widening eyes. Max's jacket had been thrown over the back of the sofa; it must have fallen out onto the floor then.

But what did she do now? Take the call and utterly confuse the caller when it was a woman rather than a man answering? Or did she just wait for it to stop ringing and hope they didn't call back?

Of course it could be Max himself, ringing in order to tell her he had dropped his mobile phone. In fact, he could have tried to reach her in the same way several times during her absence over the last twenty-four hours.

She didn't really have any choice but to answer the call, did she?

'Yes?' she prompted hesitantly, after pressing the call button.

'Max?' a female voice came back, almost as tentatively.

Well, hardly, Abby thought with a disgusted raising of her dark brows. 'Actually, no,' she answered more assuredly; she was obviously speaking to one of Max's women-friends—possibly the woman-friend of the moment. Of course, it could be his mother—but somehow she doubted that very much!

'Is this Max's phone?'

'Probably,' Abby answered dryly.

'Could I speak to Max, then?' the other woman asked coolly.

Abby drew in a deep breath. This was the tricky bit. The last person she wanted to talk to was the possibly current woman in Max's life, but at the same time she knew that he wouldn't thank her if she said anything to alienate this woman—something like, No, you can't talk to Max because he isn't here. He just happened to drop his mobile phone when he came to my apartment yesterday and made love to me!

No, Max wouldn't like that at all…

'I'm afraid he isn't here to take your call at the moment,' she answered evasively.

'Oh.' The other woman sounded disconcerted.

'But I'll be happy to tell him that you called,' she added untruthfully.

Max shouldn't even have been making love to her yesterday if he was already involved with someone else!

'I see. Right.' The other woman sounded slightly flustered. 'Okay. Perhaps you could just tell him that Kate called?'

'Just Kate?'

'Just Kate,' the other woman confirmed unhelpfully.

'Shall I tell him you'd like him to call you back?' Abby persisted.

'I think he'll know that when you give him my message,' she retorted.

There was nothing worse than someone cleverer than yourself!

Especially a female someone. 'Okay, I'll do that,' Abby managed to assure her through gritted teeth, before the other woman abruptly ended the call.

Kate.

Max was involved with someone called Kate.

She should have known. Should have guessed that a man like Max would already have someone in his life.

But she hadn't. In truth, it wasn't something she had given any thought to.

If she had she might not have allowed herself to become so attracted to him. If it was possible to control something like that, that was…

CHAPTER SIX

'YOU appear to have my mobile phone.'

She had been expecting this call, of course; Max was intelligent enough to realise that the easiest and quickest way to locate his missing mobile was to ring the number and hope someone answered it. In this case, Abby.

Oh, yes, she had been expecting this call the whole time she'd prepared her own and Monty's evening meal—chicken salad for her, chicken with rice for Monty—and as she'd cleared away the dishes and sat down to go through her notes and research on this week's guest. Mostly in the hope it would distract her from just sitting and waiting for the mobile to ring again. It hadn't succeeded, of course, but it really didn't matter; her research on the writer Barnaby Hamilton was complete, with no hidden surprises.

So, yes, she had known that Max would telephone his mobile at some point during the evening—had expected it—but she could tell by Max's derisive tone that he had already worked out that she would be the one who answered it!

'So I do,' she returned with a calm that matched his own, her hand tightly gripping the silver-coloured mobile.

'Can I come over and collect it now, or are you busy?'

She knew exactly what he meant by that last remark; he still thought, despite her denials yesterday, that Gary Holmes might be at her apartment with her this evening!

'No, I'm not busy,' she came back waspishly. 'But wouldn't it just be easier for me to post it back to you tomorrow?'

She had already given this some thought after 'Kate' had called, and, no matter how she might feel towards Max, she had decided she really wasn't up to another series of his cutting remarks. Her newly realised attraction to him, and the knowledge of Kate's presence in his life, had left her rawly exposed—so much so that she wasn't sure she could bear to see him again just yet.

'Easier for you, maybe,' he agreed dryly. 'But not as immediate. I need the mobile now, Abby. Not in two days' time,' he added firmly.

Of course he did. He was probably expecting Kate to call—probably had no idea that she had already done so!

'That sounds reasonable,' Abby returned coolly—it was the way she had decided she had to be with him if she should ever see him again—prior to finding the mobile, of course, and to Kate's call! But in these circumstances that decision applied even more.

'Oh, I'm glad about that.' He made no effort to keep the sarcasm out of his voice. 'I'll be there in half an hour.' He rang off abruptly.

'Damn him, Monty!' Abby's eyes blazed as she threw the mobile down onto her sofa, glaring at it as if it were the man himself. 'First he kisses me, then he insults me, and now he's talking to me as if I'm slightly simpleminded. Which,' she bit out self-disgustedly, 'considering I'm having a one-sided conversation with my cat, I probably am!'

Not surprising either, considering the battering her emotions had taken during the last forty-eight hours. Gary, she just wanted to strangle with her bare hands. Max…she still didn't know whether she wanted to kiss him or hit him—and at the same time knew she would do neither!

'Damn the man,' she muttered again, even as she hurried through to her bedroom to do something about her appearance.

If she had to see Max again so soon—and it appeared that she did!—then she didn't have to do it looking travel-worn and frankly less than her best. Besides, she needed an extra boost to her confidence if she was to get through this meeting with any degree of dignity at all.

She changed into stone-coloured linen trousers and a fitted brown T-shirt, freshening her make-up before brushing her shoulder-length hair until it gleamed like ebony. Slim, elegant, but not overly so, and self-possessed, she decided as she studied her reflection in the full-length mirror in her bedroom. Not bad at all. She nodded her satisfaction.

Now all she had to do was maintain that confidence in the face of Max's sarcasm—

She dropped the hairbrush she had been using on the bedroom carpet as her buzzer rang, announcing his arrival. So much for self-confidence!

She didn't even bother with the intercom, just pressing the button to let him into the building and moving to open the door seconds later as she heard the ascent of the lift.

'So much for security,' he rasped, totally ignoring the

mobile she held out to him as he strode past her into the apartment. 'You could have been letting in a serial rapist for all you knew!' he added harshly.

Abby closed the door gently behind him. 'Or worse—one of those religious fanatics,' she returned, dark brows raised mockingly.

He looked—wonderful, she thought, aching. Black denims, black T-shirt beneath a brown leather jacket, his dark hair windswept.

His expression, as usual, was guarded as his gaze swept over her own appearance with the same nonchalance. 'Or a religious fanatic,' he agreed, some of the tension leaving his shoulders. 'Not that I have anything against religion. I just don't like it appearing uninvited on my doorstep.'

Abby, in the circumstances of her father actually being a vicar, had no intention of commenting on the subject. 'Yours, I believe.' She held out the mobile to him once again.

He took it, his fingers lightly brushing hers, before slipping the mobile into his jacket pocket. 'Where did you find it?'

She shrugged, moving away from the intensity of his gaze. 'It must have fallen out of your jacket pocket yesterday, when you threw it on the sofa.'

'When *I* threw it on the sofa?' Max repeated huskily.

She had been hoping he wouldn't bring up the subject of that time in his arms yesterday—or the fact that *she* had been the one to remove his jacket in order to be closer to the warmth of his chest and arms.

She should have known he wasn't the sort of man to avoid any subject. As long as it wasn't one *he* wanted to avoid, of course!

Her chin rose challengingly as she met his gaze. 'You had a phone call earlier.'

'Yes.' He nodded, unmoving, his gaze as steady and unyielding as hers.

He knew Kate had called!

And the only way he could know that was if the other woman also had the number of his land-line—or had actually gone to his apartment to see him in person. In order to ask him who the woman was who had answered his mobile? *Oh, what a tangled web we weave…*

But that wasn't Abby's problem, was it? Okay, so she had been the one to throw off his jacket, and consequently cause his mobile to fall out of the pocket, but if Max hadn't been kissing her at the time, touching her so that she needed to touch him in return—

'From a woman called Kate,' she went on—she was sure unnecessarily.

Max's mouth tightened grimly, his gaze once again guarded. 'She told me.'

How had she told him? In person? Was the other woman at his apartment even now, waiting for him to come back to her…?

No! She wouldn't do this! She was thinking and acting like a jealous lover where Max was concerned. Something that after only a few kisses she had no right to do. No matter how much she might wish it were otherwise…

Abby thrust her shaking hands into the pockets of her linen trousers. 'Don't let me keep you,' she told him tightly.

He completely ignored her dismissal as he moved to sit in one of the armchairs, looking up at her thoughtfully. 'You seem a little—tense?'

Her frown was pained now. She'd had the impression

this would only be a quick visit on Max's part—to collect his mobile and then leave. But he seemed to be making himself comfortable.

She shrugged. 'We didn't exactly part on a happy note yesterday,' she reminded him tautly. 'In fact, I had the distinct impression you hoped never to see me again!'

'Did you?' His gaze softened, unnerving after his earlier stiltedness. 'And yet here I am,' he added. 'Hello, boy,' he greeted Monty ruefully as the cat jumped up onto his lap and began to purr for attention.

Attention he received. One of Max's sensuously long hands began to stroke the long silky fur on the cat's back, causing Monty to arch in pleasure, his expression ecstatic.

In the same way that she had when Max had caressed her?

God, this was just too embarrassing; every thought she had seemed to come straight back to Max. It was devastating to realise she was so attracted to him she couldn't think of anything else.

Why him? she groaned inwardly. Why was she so enraptured with this arrogantly aloof man, who pushed her away one second and pulled her into his arms the next, and not with some nice, uncomplicated man like Andrew, who had wanted to marry her and have lots of children, be the father of the grandchildren her parents had begun painfully to hint that they would like?

Max Harding wasn't that sort of man, and he never would be.

She shook her head. 'I really think you should go now, don't you?'

A smile still curved his lips as he looked up from

stroking a now settled Monty. 'I thought you said you weren't busy this evening?'

'I'm not—but you probably are!' she said forcefully. Exasperatedly. He had his mobile—why didn't he just go?

He shrugged. 'Not particularly.'

She was going to make a complete idiot of herself in a minute and say something embarrassing—for herself, that was. She doubted that there was very much that embarrassed Max.

'I thought perhaps you had to get back to Kate?' She said it anyway, at the same time refusing to drop her gaze from his suddenly narrowed eyes.

'Did you?' he finally said slowly.

'For God's sake, will you stop answering a question with another question?' Abby's control snapped impatiently, her movements agitated.

Max arched dark brows. 'Am I doing that?'

'You just did it again!' she snapped. 'And if you answer a question with another question you give no answer whatsoever. It's an art you've obviously perfected,' she added derisively.

He was frowning darkly now, his movements studied as he placed Monty on one of the cushions of the sofa and stood up before turning to face her. 'Maybe I was a little hard on you before I left here yesterday—'

'You weren't "hard", Max—you were brutally honest!' she corrected tightly, blue eyes glittering with humiliated memory. 'But then,' she added slightly bitterly, 'why should I have expected anything else from the great, the talented, the acerbic Max Harding?'

Was she going too far? Probably. But she was too angry, too hurt, to defensive about her own feelings for him to be anything else.

He sighed his frustration. 'I'm not someone you should become involved with, Abby—'

'I'm not involved with you,' she interrupted, knowing she lied. How she lied!

'—and, no matter how I might wish it were otherwise, you aren't someone I can become involved with, either,' Max finished.

She became very still, frowning across at him, finding that last remark enigmatic in the extreme. What did he mean, she wasn't someone he could become involved with?

In a sense, the two of them were already involved—their lives were entangled even if their emotions—Max's, at least—weren't. They each knew where the other lived, they had lunched together, had a mutual friend in Dorothy. Their lives might never have crossed before, but now that they had it was unlikely they would never do so again. In fact, feeling about him as she did, Abby hoped they would!

She raised dark brows. 'Are we back to your friend Kate again?' It was difficult for her to keep her voice even and unemotional.

Max's breath hissed harshly through his teeth. 'I would like you to forget that you ever took her call—'

'I'll just bet you would!' Abby came back incredulously, shaking her head. 'You keep your relationship with her pretty quiet, don't you, Max?' she challenged. 'No being seen out together. No photographs of the two of you in the newspapers. No—

'My God!' she gasped as a sudden thought occurred to her. 'She's not married, is she?' she asked belatedly, more disappointed than shocked.

She wasn't a prude, despite having a vicar for a father, and knew that even if her guess was right, Max would be far from the first man to have an affair with a married woman. The difference was, she wasn't attracted to any of those other men!

'So the great, the legendary Max Harding, is having an affair with a married woman!' she said scathingly.

Max didn't move so much as a muscle, and yet he suddenly seemed bigger, more powerful, more—dangerous!

Yes, that was exactly how he now appeared, Abby realised with a slightly dazed blink. His eyes were glittering furiously, his face grimly challenging, every muscle in that tightly hewn body tensed as if ready to spring. At her? Because she had guessed his secret? But why should it matter so much that he was involved with a married woman? After all, he wasn't the first, and she was pretty sure he wouldn't be the last either.

'This,' he finally bit out with cold derision, 'coming from a woman who hasn't been in her own apartment for the last twenty-four hours! Oh, yes, Abby, I know you've been out all night,' he taunted her, as her expression turned to one of astonishment. 'You see, I missed my mobile some time yesterday evening, so I rang it to see who answered. No one answered. Not last night. Not this morning. Not early this afternoon either.' His mouth twisted. 'Monty wasn't the only one 'out on the tiles' all night!'

Abby stared at him. The conclusions that Max had come to concerning her absence were simply incredible. Okay, so she was twenty-seven years old, unattached and not unattractive—but did that really mean that the only reason she could possibly have been out all night was because she had spent it with a man? Obviously to Max it did.

'As this is the middle of London, Monty doesn't actually go out on the tiles,' she began, knowing her pet's reticence had nothing to do with safety and everything to do with the fact that all his creature comforts were right here. 'And, as it happens,' she continued determinedly as Max tried to speak, 'neither do I! In fact,' she added firmly as her resolve deepened, 'I think the implication is just a clever attempt on your part to distract my attention from your relationship with Kate. How frustrating it must be for you that the two of us talked on the telephone earlier—'

'I think you should stop right there, Abby!' Max cut in icily, his expression grimmer than ever—dangerously so.

Abby refused to back down, just as she refused to let her gaze drop from his cold eyes. 'I think you should just take your mobile and leave.'

He gave a frustrated sigh. 'There's just no reasoning with you, is there?'

'Reasoning, yes. Sheer bloody arrogance, no! I get all the arrogance I can take working with the conceited Gary Holmes,' she added challengingly. And after the accusations Max had made yesterday, and his comments now concerning her absence from her apartment last night, he could make what he liked of that remark!

But there was no telling what he *did* think about it. Max's expression became remotely unreadable just at the mention of the other man's name. 'I would rather not talk about Gary Holmes. And I would prefer it if you didn't discuss my private life with him either.'

'I don't know anything *about* your private life!' Except the brief—very brief—part she had played in it. And about Kate, of course…

Abby gave him a searching look. Was she the 'private life' he was referring to? And, if so, what possible interest could this woman Kate be to Gary Holmes?

Unless the other man knew Kate? Who she was? Whose wife she was?

'Don't even go there, Abby,' Max warned darkly, seeming to easily read her thoughts from her expression.

She had never been good at hiding her emotions; it probably came from being the only child of loving parents who had always encouraged her to believe that honesty was the best policy. Because in her parents' world—in her own world until she was twenty-one and left university—it had been. It was only since she had entered the world of politics and television that she had discovered the truth usually had very little to do with anything. Cynical, perhaps, but it was a lesson she had learnt during the last six years—and learnt it well.

She met Max's gaze unflinchingly. 'I have no idea what you're talking about.'

'I'm warning you, Abby—'

'Threats now, Max?' she taunted lightly, shaking her head. 'Not a good way to divert an interviewer's interest away from a possible story!'

'There *is* no story.'

'Isn't there?' Abby returned tightly. 'You're very emotional about something you claim is unimportant—' She broke off as Max stepped forward to grasp her arms and glare down at her fiercely, his face mere inches away from hers, the warmth of his breath stirring the ragged tendrils of hair on her forehead.

Her first wide-eyed thought was that he was going to shake her until her teeth rattled. Her second was that he was going to kiss her insensible.

The second thought was the correct one.

And it didn't take him too long to do it, either.

Mere seconds after Max had taken her into his arms, his mouth taking fierce possession of hers, Abby had totally forgotten everything but that—was aware of nothing but Max and the desire that glared between them unchecked.

It was as if no time had elapsed between yesterday afternoon and tonight. And maybe it hadn't. Their passion seemed to rage to fever-pitch in seconds.

Abby had no idea, no memory, of going into her bedroom—only knew they must have left a trail of clothes on their way there, since both of them were naked by the time they fell on top of the bedclothes, hands seeking, mouths locked hungrily.

Max's body was just as she remembered it from that first day: lean and hard, covered with fine, silky dark hair, thicker on his chest and down his stomach. His back was wide and muscled, tapering to powerful thighs and long, athletic legs—legs that became entangled with hers as she lay back on the bed.

His dark head bent and his lips claimed the pouting arousal of her breasts. Her body arched as she gasped with pleasure. Max's mouth was hotly moist, his tongue caressing, teeth gently biting, sending rivers of molten pleasure coursing deeply between her thighs. One of his hands was caressing her there, seeking and finding the centre of her pleasure, his lightest touch sending her completely over the edge. The pleasure was everywhere now, inside her, hot, wet, totally mind-blowing.

But there was no time to even catch her breath as Max's mouth moved back to claim hers, tongues duelling, hands seeking, finding. Abby felt Max shudder with pleasure as she touched his hardness, hot and throbbing, guiding him now as he sought to join his body with hers.

He filled her totally, possessed her as he moved inside her with long, slow strokes that quickly aroused her already sensitised flesh to a second climax, her body convulsing about his, threatening to take him with her.

He became still above her, delaying the moment, lips and hands once more caressing. Abby's hands moved restlessly across his back, nails raking the skin there, feeling the way he quivered beneath those caresses, knowing his self-control was reaching breaking point.

And she wanted it to—wanted to feel his own shuddering release, to know that she had pleasured him as he had pleasured her.

And then his movements were no longer slow, his hips pulsing against hers, taking her with him. Their moment of release was completely simultaneous, with Abby no longer sure where Max began and she ended, only able to cling to Max in an effort not to be completely swept away by the tidal wave.

'My God…!' Max groaned as he looked down at her with dark, heated eyes before burying his face in her throat.

My God, indeed. Abby had never dreamt, never known… It was true—love did make a difference!

And she loved Max. Deeply, strongly. In fact, nothing else mattered but the deep love she now realised she felt for him.

It was dark when she woke, some time later, briefly disorientated by the knowledge of another presence. Then, as Max sat up and quietly moved to the other side of her bed, it all came back to her in a warm rush of well-being:

their incredible lovemaking, being held in Max's arms afterwards, her head resting on his shoulder as he cradled her against him and they both drifted off to sleep.

Max hadn't commented on it last night—and she hoped he never would—but he had been her first lover.

She wasn't a prude—hadn't lacked opportunities either. And of course there had been Andrew. It was just that she had been brought up to believe that love, not curiosity, was the only reason for making love with someone—that the body as well as the emotions was a precious gift, not to be given lightly.

But until Max she had never been in love…

And, being the newly awoken lover that she was, even in her sleep she'd been completely attuned to Max's slightest movement—knowing the moment his arms left her and the warmth of his body was removed from her side. She turned her head on the pillow now, to look at the broad expanse of his back reflected in the moonlight from the undrawn curtains at the window. But he didn't move, simply sat there, seeming unaware that she was awake.

'What are you doing?' Even her voice sounded different in her knowledge of what it was to make love: softer, more sensual.

Max turned sharply, his face all shadows in the moonlight, his eyes unreadable. 'I didn't mean to wake you.'

Abby shook her head, her hair darkly tangled on the pillow beneath her. From the wild caress of Max's hands, she remembered warmly.

'You didn't.' She smiled, stretching her newly awakened body. Every ache was a pleasurable one. Even the bruises she was sure would be on her shoulders from the pressure of Max's fingers as their desire had spiralled out of control were something to be cherished and held to her. Like battle scars. Except these were love scars…

'What are you doing?' she repeated more urgently as Max stood up and began to pull on the items of clothing—denims, and boxer shorts—that littered the bedroom carpet.

He zipped his jeans over perfect hips before answering her. 'Leaving you to get some more sleep.'

'But—'

'I need to get home to shower and change; I have an early appointment this morning, Abby.' He moved to sit on her side of the bed, reaching down to caress the hair from her face, smoothing the frown from between her eyes with the pad of his thumb. 'I'll call you later, okay?'

No, it was not okay. She didn't want him to leave, didn't want to go back to sleep, wanted the two of them to make love again. And again. And again. She wanted Max to stay!

Her absolute certainty from last night, of loving and being loved, began to fade in the increasing daylight in the bedroom. Max's expression revealed nothing of what he did or didn't feel towards her. Last night had been incredible, a revelation to Abby, but she could see none of that reflected in Max's face. In fact, his expression was once again totally unreadable.

Abby felt like crying.

Max looked at her searchingly for several long seconds, and then he was gone from the side of the bed, standing up forcefully. 'I will call you, Abby.'

'When?' she asked—and despised herself for doing so. She sounded like someone clinging to a man who didn't want to be clung to.

'Later,' he promised harshly, before turning away to

stride into the other room—probably in order to collect the rest of his abandoned clothes.

Abby's instinct was to follow him—an instinct she instantly resisted, instead lying unmoving in the bed, her hearing acutely attuned as she heard Max dressing, talking briefly to Monty, heard her apartment door opening and then closing softly seconds later.

Max had gone.

After sharing with her the most beautiful, memorable experience, he had simply dressed and left.

Because last night hadn't meant the same to him as it had to her?

The tears began to fall then, hot rivers of them, scouring and burning as deeply as the love she now felt for Max.

Love. A word, she realised with painful hindsight, that had never passed Max's lips.

CHAPTER SEVEN

'HAS anyone ever told you you're an extremely difficult woman to find?'

Abby glanced up from the sheets of information strewn across the desk in front of her, no welcome in her expression as she watched Gary Holmes stroll into the room uninvited to perch on the edge of her desk, boyishly handsome.

'Do you mind?' she snapped, looking at him pointedly as he sat on some of the papers she had been reading. Or at least attempting to read.

It was an effort to distract herself from thinking about Max and his abrupt departure this morning. Not that it was working at the moment. For her there was nothing except Max.

Even though it had only been five-thirty when he'd left, she hadn't slept after he had gone. Her year of working on breakfast television had disciplined her into waking early and alert; it was a habit she hadn't yet managed to shake off, and Max's sudden departure had completely robbed her of any desire for further sleep anyway.

So she had got up instead, drinking several cups of coffee as she'd prowled her apartment, no longer sure, as the agonising minutes had passed, what had happened between herself and Max.

The more she'd thought about it the more she had come to realise that although Max might have made love with her, he had certainly never said he was *in* love with her—not even during those most intimate moments.

And the more convinced she had become that he was not going to call her later, either.

She had, in fact, become that well-worn cliché, a one-night stand. Her own feelings of love towards Max had just blinded her to that fact.

Until that moment.

She had left her apartment, the scene of her naïveté, like one pursued, rushing to the office she shared with her researchers, glad no one else was in yet as she tried to bury herself in the extensive notes she needed to go through before her programme on Friday evening.

A wasted effort so far. She had no interest in her guest or in the programme, couldn't concentrate on the words written in front of her as thoughts intruded again and again of what had happened the previous night— seeking a balm, anything to salve her cringing humiliation. And finding none.

Gary Holmes, grinning at her cheerfully as he pushed the papers to one side and sat down again, was the last person she wanted to see just now!

His blue eyes narrowed thoughtfully as he looked down at her, almost as if he sensed there was something different about her...

Was there? she wondered, slightly panicked. Did the sort of mind-blowing, sense-filling lovemaking she and Max had shared the night before leave some sort of physical mark for others to see? She hoped not!

She stood up abruptly, moving restlessly to stand in front of the window, her expression shadowed by the sunlight streaming in behind her. 'What do you want, Gary?' she snapped.

Her annoyance was completely wasted on the thick-skinned Gary, and he returned her hostile gaze unperturbed. 'You aren't exactly being nice, Abby. All I've ever wanted was to be your friend.'

Abby gave a scornful laugh; she must have missed that particular conversation! All Gary had ever done was ridicule and belittle her. 'You haven't succeeded!'

'No?' He raised blond brows, his expression thoughtful for a few seconds before he shrugged. 'Maybe you're right,' he agreed without concern. 'But it isn't too late for us to start again?' he added with throaty flirtation.

'Start again?' she repeated. 'And just what have I done to merit this generous offer on your part?' Her eyes glittered with challenge.

He was openly grinning now. 'I may not have liked you very much to begin with, Abby—'

'What a surprise!' She shook her head. 'The feeling, I can assure you, is still mutual.' She had no intention of even *trying* to be polite to this man after the mischief he had deliberately tried to create for her on Saturday.

Initially she had tried, in the face of great provocation, to maintain a professional respect for this man's obvious brilliance as a director, but over the last few days he had been the one to step over the line of that working relationship and into her private life. There, she owed him no respect whatsoever.

'Just what did you think you were doing, coming to my apartment in that way on Saturday?' she demanded.

He shrugged. 'Believe it or not, trying to save you from yourself.' He looked at her with narrowed eyes. 'But perhaps I'm too late to do that…?' he said slowly.

Something about her *was* different, Abby realized, and embarrassed colour stained her cheeks. She had no idea what it could be, what it was that Gary could see that she couldn't, but he knew. It was written there in his scathingly pitying expression; he *knew* she and Max were lovers.

The scorn she could understand—Gary seemed to feel that way about most emotional relationships—but why the pity?

Her gaze didn't quite meet his now. 'I have no idea what you're talking about.'

'Don't you?' he came back quickly. 'Oh, I think you do, Abby.' The colour drained from her cheeks as quickly as it had stained them, and Gary shook his head. 'You're playing with the big boys now.'

'I'm not playing at all,' she snapped, wondering, after her recent humiliation, just how much more of this she could take.

He nodded. 'And that's going to be your problem.' He made himself more comfortable on the desktop. 'Max is a major league player, and you're nothing but a lightweight. In other words, Abby, he'll crush you like a bug that's unwittingly stepped into his path.'

She gave another shake of her head, trembling slightly now, having already come to the same conclusion herself not so long ago. 'Isn't that my business?'

'Not if it's going to affect the programme, no,' Gary rasped. 'As I said, you're a lightweight who should never have been put in this position, but—'

'That's only *your* opinion,' she cut in forcefully,

stung beyond measure that he was repeating Max's words from their very first meeting.

That seemed so very long ago now. So much had happened—and yet in reality it was only a matter of days.

'My professional as well as my personal opinion,' Gary continued remorselessly, a man confident of his own professional worth. 'So, to recap: you're a lightweight, but unfortunately you happen to be the principal in my latest programme. It's in my interest to see that you don't self-destruct.'

'And you believe my seeing Max Harding is going to result in that?' she said scornfully. 'I'm still trying to persuade him into appearing on the show, Gary. Or had you forgotten that?' She tossed back the darkness of her shoulder-length hair.

He gave her another pitying glance. 'How have you been doing so far?'

Not well, she inwardly acknowledged. In fact, she hadn't even given that aspect of their relationship a thought during the last twenty-four hours!

'An open channel of dialogue is a vast improvement on his total non-compliance of a week ago,' she defended evasively.

'Has he agreed to appear on the programme?'

'I told you, I'm still—'

'Has Max Harding agreed to appear on the programme?' Gary repeated through gritted teeth, all mockery gone now, his eyes glittering intently.

She swallowed hard. 'Not yet. But that doesn't mean—'

'He isn't going to.' Gary ignored her protest. 'Not now. Not ever. But don't take it personally, Abby,' he added with some of his earlier derision. 'Max Harding will never appear unscripted on public television again. He daren't. Because he can't take the risk of being questioned about his private life.'

Abby became very still, her expression guarded now. 'What about his private life?' So far she and the researchers had managed to find out very little about that—just normal background stuff, such as parents, education, television credits. The private side of Max's personal life remained exactly that. Private.

Except, she thought dully, last night probably made *her* a part of that private life…

Gary gave her an exasperated look. 'Did you never wonder why Rory Mayhew chose Max's programme to attempt to commit suicide?'

'The man's life was in tatters,' she came back impatiently. 'His political career was in ruins, totally beyond repair after that property scandal. He had only that day been forced into resigning from his government post. It was also rumoured that his wife was leaving him because of an affair—'

'Yes,' Gary put in softly, the full weight of innuendo behind that one word.

Abby looked at him dazedly. She was tired from lack of sleep, upset beyond measure at Max's casual 'I'll call you later'—how many other women had he said that to before never contacting them again?—and just too emotionally fragile to make any sense of whatever Gary was implying.

She shook her head. 'I don't see how any of that has anything to do with Max.'

'No?' Gary gave her another pitying look. 'That rather depends on which of the Mayhews was having the affair, doesn't it? And who with,' he added softly.

Abby stared at him unblinkingly for several long seconds, and then she finally realised exactly what he was saying.

She didn't believe it!

Rory Mayhew's professional life had been over so far as politics were concerned—absolutely no going back on that. The bribes and deals he had arranged during his brief time in government, and the added rumours of the total collapse of his private life had been enough to drive any man to the point of suicide.

Something he had achieved on his second time of trying…

The shamed politician had been seen by a doctor following his behaviour on the Max Harding show, but must have given quite a convincing performance of sanity, because he had been released from medical supervision only two days later. At which time he had booked into an obscure hotel and downed the contents of a bottle of pills, washing them down with whisky.

There had been no Max Harding on hand to stop him that time.

But now Gary seemed to be implying something else about that whole incident. Something totally unbelievable.

She gave a denying movement of her head. 'Rory Mayhew was the one having an affair—'

'Was he?' Gary's smile was completely confident. 'Or was that just something that gained credence once the man was dead? After all—' his mouth twisted derisively '—his reputation was already beyond repair. And—what's the saying?—you have to protect the living…'

What he was implying, what he was saying, was that it had been Rory Mayhew's *wife* who had been having an affair. And that the man involved was Max.

'You don't have to believe me, Abby.'

'I don't!' she said, with more determination than actual conviction.

Because she didn't know!

The whole incident had taken place two years ago, at a time when she had been trying to pursue her own career. Oh, she had seen the programme, had been as shocked as the rest of the general public and had read all the scandalous details that had followed in the newspapers. But she, like everyone else, had only ever known what the press chose to tell her. She didn't really know what had happened, why it was that Rory Mayhew should have felt desperate enough to attempt suicide on television.

'Don't you, Abby?' Gary taunted as he saw her doubts. 'She was in his life then, and she's still in his life now,' he added softly.

Her lashes fluttered uncertainly. She couldn't meet his gaze. 'Who is?'

'Kate Mayhew, of course.'

'Kate?' Abby echoed sharply, clearly remembering Max's excuses about the woman Kate who had telephoned, and his reaction to her suggestion that the other woman might be married. 'Kate Mayhew?'

Was that the reason Max had made love to her? Because he had hoped to distract her attention from his relationship with the woman she knew only as Kate?

No, she couldn't believe that—wouldn't believe that of Max. Gary was just being his usual vindictive self. If only she didn't feel so vulnerable. If only she felt more sure of her own relationship with Max!

Gary was looking at her speculatively now. 'You've obviously heard the name.' He nodded his satisfaction.

'But not from Max, I'm sure. Max likes to play things close to his chest on that particular subject. He'll do anything he can to hide the fact that he's still involved with Kate Mayhew.'

So the woman who'd called had had the same name—that didn't prove anything. Did it?

'How do you know so much about him?' Abby attacked.

'Didn't he tell you?' Gary smiled, standing up. 'I was the director on *The Max Harding Forum* two years ago. So you see, Abby,' he continued mercilessly at her stunned silence, 'I'm in a position to know *exactly* what happened. In fact, if you decide you want to know any more about it, I suggest you come and ask me.' He swung the door open. 'Max, I'm sure, will never tell you or anyone else the truth about what happened,' he concluded with certainty, closing the door softly behind him as he left.

Abby couldn't move. Couldn't breathe.

Gary had been the director on Max's show two years ago? Was *that* the reason for the antagonism between the two men?

What did it matter what the reason was for their dislike of each other? None of that told her what she really wanted—needed—to know. And that was the truth about the Mayhews. What had really happened two years ago. Whether Kate Mayhew was the Kate from the phone call! Because, if she was, that put a whole different light on Max's continuing friendship with her...

But until she did know—and she was far too familiar with how much Gary enjoyed being malicious!—she was more inclined to believe the man she loved than Gary's vicious lies.

Although that didn't stop her sense of unease every time she thought of the possibility of the woman Kate being Rory Mayhew's widow…

'Dinner tonight, Abby?'

This had not been the best day of her life—in fact, Abby couldn't remember a worse one!

She had spent most of it, after Gary had left, fluctuating between believing totally in Max and their own relationship, and doubts concerning his evasion where that call from Kate was concerned.

She was still inclined to believe that Gary had it all wrong, and that the woman who had telephoned Max wasn't Kate Mayhew at all—after all, Kate really wasn't an uncommon name—but every time she decided that she remembered Max's behaviour over the call, his refusal to discuss it or the woman called Kate.

She had arrived home ten minutes ago, literally feeling like something Monty had dragged in, and really hadn't been prepared, emotionally or in any other way, for Max's telephone call.

'Abby?' Max prompted now at her continued silence. 'If you would rather not go out I can always come over there, and we can order something in—'

'No!' She felt compelled to reject that idea; she had no idea how this evening was going to turn out, and knew that in spite of herself she was still disturbed by her conversation with Gary earlier. Even if that was probably what he had intended all along. 'Why don't I bring some food over to your apartment and we can cook there?' she went on hastily. 'That way you won't have to get up and leave in the morning.' She couldn't stop herself from adding that. His sudden departure this morning still rankled.

Even if he *had* now called, as he had said he would…

'It's been a while, Abby,' he remarked wryly.

'What has?' she came back warily, desperately wishing she didn't feel so uncertain—of Max, of their own relationship. Because if she hadn't she would have been able to tell Gary to take his accusations and innuendos and—

'Abby?' Max questioned sharply now, obviously sensing that something was wrong.

How she wished she could behave differently. How she *wanted* to behave differently! But the truth was she felt battered and bruised—from Max's sudden departure this morning, from her hateful conversation with Gary Holmes later—and was hating the fact that her uncertainties about her own relationship with Max had succeeded in putting doubts into her mind.

'Abby, have I upset you with the way I left this morning?' Max pursued gruffly. 'I told you, I'm a little rusty at this sort of thing. I didn't mean to upset you by leaving the way I did, but I really did have an early appointment.'

At five-thirty in the morning? Somehow she very much doubted that! Unless it had been with the lovely Kate? And if that Kate *was* Kate Mayhew, then she *was* lovely, Abby knew, having managed to find several photographs on file of the tall, beautiful redhead. Now thirty-five, the mother of two young children, Abby also knew that Kate Mayhew had not remarried…

'I'm not upset, Max,' she told him. 'I've been working all day, I only got in ten minutes ago, and I'm tired—that's all.'

'Sure?' His voice had deepened to husky intimacy, causing a quiver of awareness down Abby's spine as it brought sharply back into focus all the intimacies they had shared the previous night.

'I'm sure,' she told him with brisk determination, shaking off that awareness. For self-preservation's sake, if nothing else! 'Look, just give me an hour to shower and change, and I'll come over with some food.'

'Forget the food. Just bring yourself,' Max told her gruffly. 'If we get hungry for food later we can order something in.'

Later. Implying they would be occupied doing something else when she first arrived. And Abby wasn't naïve enough not to know what that something would be.

But she needed to be a lot more certain of him than she was to withstand a second battering to her emotions...

'I haven't eaten all day, Max.' She had been too busy to even think about food! 'I need feeding before I do anything else.'

There was the briefest of pauses before he replied, 'Okay. I'll uncork some wine and have it waiting for when you get here.'

A whole bottle of it to herself, Abby decided as she rang off and moved lethargically towards the bathroom. Preferably with a straw!

She shouldn't be doing this—shouldn't be going anywhere near Max when she was so filled with questions and doubts about the two of them continuing to see each other.

Oh, stop lying to yourself, Abby, she told herself disgustedly. She wanted to see Max again, *needed* to see him. She loved him, for goodness' sake! And once she was with him all Gary's lies, his insinuations, would evaporate, she was sure.

CHAPTER EIGHT

'I was beginning to think you had changed your mind,' Max greeted her huskily an hour and a half later, as he let her into his apartment.

In truth, she had. Several times, in fact. Her emotions had fluctuated between wanting to see Max, to be with him and the other extreme of wondering why he had made love to her last night—whether it was because he loved her as she loved him, or for some other reason.

She needed to see him again tonight if only to try and find the answer to that. All the time hoping it was because he loved her!

'Did you?' She moved on tiptoe to lightly brush her lips against his. 'Dinner.' She held up the bag she carried, looking at him beneath from under lashes.

He looked ruggedly handsome in a black silk shirt and faded black denims, his feet once again bare; obviously it was a trait of his when in the privacy of his apartment. Or else it was his way of having less clothing to remove later…

Oh, God!

Just looking at him made her feel weak at the knees. Not only did she know Max intimately, but he knew her in the same way—much more so than any other man. And without any declaration of love, from either of them, how could she help but feel a certain amount of shyness and uncertainty now that she was with him again?

Gary Holmes and his insinuations could just go to hell—she had enough insecurities of her own concerning this relationship without wondering if there was any truth in what he had said!

It was taking every ounce of self-confidence she had to face Max again this evening. In fact, with Max looking at her so broodingly, she suddenly wished she'd inherited some of her mother's undoubted acting ability; she might at least have been able to pretend a semblance of sophistication then. As it was, she had absolutely no idea how to behave with this man who was her lover!

She smiled at him brightly. 'Shall I take the food through to the kitchen?' She didn't wait for his reply before turning and doing exactly that. 'I brought steak, potatoes, and the makings of a salad,' she continued as she unpacked the food, desperately hoping to hide her increasing tension.

Max's next comment proved she hadn't succeeded. *Sorry, Mum!*

'What's happened, Abby?'

She opened wide cornflower-blue eyes. 'Happened?' she repeated with a puzzled glance.

Max was standing only inches away now, his expression more brooding than ever. 'You seem—different.'

Well, of course she was different! She was no longer a twenty-seven-year-old virgin, but this man's lover. And she had no idea and no experience of how to behave in a situation like this!

'In what way do you feel I'm different this evening?'

she asked casually. 'If you mean I seem a little tense, then you're probably right. Unlike you, Max, I'm not just a little rusty; this is all new to me.'

'Do you think I don't know that?' he murmured huskily, moving forward to take her into his arms, his gaze intent on her face. 'Why me, Abby?'

He had known he was her first lover. That just made it all the more embarrassing. Max was thirty-nine, obviously a man of experience, and probably found it incredible that she had actually been a virgin. And, having no idea how he felt towards her, she could hardly come out with a declaration of love, now, could she?

She smiled, determined to salvage some of her shaky pride; after all, she was in her late twenties, not an immature schoolgirl. 'Why not you?' she came back flippantly. 'I always was a late developer, but every girl has to start somewhere!'

His gaze was searching now. A gaze Abby withstood with effort.

Max shook his head. 'If you had told me I would have been more—gentle.'

He had been 'gentle' enough for her to fall more deeply in love with him than ever!

'Why didn't *you*—' she poked a friendly finger into his chest '—tell me that Gary Holmes was the director on your programme two years ago?' Changing the subject, even to one as unpleasant as Gary Holmes, seemed like a good idea at that moment.

A shutter came down over Max's features, telling her of his sudden tension. 'You've talked to Holmes today?' he said harshly.

'Well, of course I've talked to Gary today; he's the director of my show too, you know,' Abby came back lightly—perhaps she did have some of her mother's act-ing ability after all?

She certainly didn't want to be having this seem-ingly playful conversation with Max. What she really wanted to do was scream and shout, to cry, to demand he tell her exactly what was going on, to pummel the hard width of his chest with her fists as she felt he was pummelling her heart.

Max's arm dropped from about her waist and he stepped back, his expression wary now. 'And what else did he have to say?'

She shrugged. 'You know Gary—as acerbic as ever.'

Max's mouth thinned. 'Exactly what did he say to you, Abby?' he rasped harshly.

Her mouth twisted. 'Just his usual bluster, really. Mainly directed at the fact that I'll never persuade you into appearing on my show. But then, I already know that, don't I?' she added with a casualness she was far from feeling. 'Look, could we start cooking dinner now? I really am hungry.' Every mouthful would probably choke her, but she was determined to get through this.

Because, if she were to salvage anything from this relationship at all, it was becoming increasingly obvi-ous that she needed to know what had really happened two years ago. Was still happening?

Max seemed to shake himself out of his sudden tension with effort, taking the steaks from her to begin preparing them for grilling. 'I think I now understand the reason why you aren't in the best of moods this evening,' he remarked lightly. 'Gary Holmes used to have that effect on me too!'

Abby turned away to wash the potatoes. 'You still haven't told me why you didn't mention he had been your director,' she prompted.

Max grimaced. 'Gary Holmes, and working with him, are things I've tried to block out of my mind.'

It wasn't exactly an answer. Any more than Gary's attitude towards Max had been explained by either of them. But it was obvious the two men disliked each other intensely, and it was yet another riddle Abby felt she had to get to the bottom of.

'Here, let's have a glass of wine—' Max poured them both a glass of the red wine he'd uncorked '—and forget all about Gary Holmes.'

She only wished that she could, Abby acknowledged as she obligingly sipped the delicious wine. But no matter how she tried she simply couldn't forget the awful things Gary had said to her.

'How did your meeting go this morning?' she asked, once they were sitting down to eat their meal.

Max had prepared the table in the dining-room before she'd arrived, with silver cutlery and lighted candles. Very romantic. Except Abby didn't feel very romantic. What she really felt was an inexperienced fool. And fools, she knew, made bad company. Hence her less that scintillating conversation.

How much different this could have been, she cried inwardly. If she hadn't already felt upset by Max's sudden departure this morning. If Gary hadn't poured his vitriol into her ears.

She could see by Max's rueful expression that he was less than satisfied with the way the evening was going too.

'Not very well,' he answered her, sipping his wine. 'I spent the best part of two hours over a mediocre breakfast, convincing a man that I'm not interested in having my biography written and that at thirty-nine I'm only halfway through my life, not at the end of it.' He grimaced. 'No doubt he'll go ahead and write an unauthorised version, anyway.'

'A biography?' Abby's interest quickened. 'Now, that *would* be interesting,' she said slowly. Very interesting!

Max gave her a reproachful grin. 'If I'm not interested in appearing on a half-hour chat show, I'm certainly not interested in seeing a book about myself!'

She kept her lashes down in order to hide the sudden flare of hurt in her eyes.

That had been very neatly done. Too neatly. Letting her know that nothing had changed with regard to appearing on her show, but doing it without actually antagonising her. Because he still had the woman Kate to protect! That knowledge had nothing to do with anything Gary Holmes had told her this morning about the other woman's full identity—she still didn't trust him!—and everything to do with Max's own attitude with regard to the other woman.

And that would hurt no matter what Gary had said to her. She and Max were lovers, and yet there was another woman in his life called Kate that he refused to talk about. Not exactly reassuring to any new lover, was it?

How many other women in the last two years had wondered about Max's friendship with the other woman, too? And how many of those relationships had floundered because of it?

More to the point, why was Max so secretive about the relationship?

The answer to that, if the woman really *was* Kate Mayhew, was all too easy to guess, Abby realised painfully; any public relationship between Kate Mayhew and Max Harding after the scandal two years ago would dredge it up all over again—perhaps even lead to speculation concerning exactly what their relationship might have been then.

In the same position, Abby felt she would say to hell with it and let the media do their worst. The fact that Max and Kate hadn't only seemed to confirm that they had something to hide…

'This evening isn't going too well, is it?' Max rasped suddenly, giving up all pretence of eating his own meal and pushing the plate away.

If he hadn't left so abruptly this morning… If Gary hadn't told her the things he had, causing her concerns to become full-blown doubts… Abby knew it would all have been so different then, that instead of being on the defensive, guarded in her words and actions, she would probably have behaved like a simpering lovestruck idiot. In retrospect, perhaps this was better. More painful, maybe, but better.

Her gaze was still guarded as she looked across at him. 'We don't know each other very well, that's all,' she said, with an attempt at unconcern.

He frowned darkly. 'That didn't seem to bother either of us last night.'

Sadly, despite everything, Abby knew it wouldn't bother her if he were to take her in his arms again now either.

'Perhaps that's the problem?' she suggested lightly. 'We jumped ten steps ahead of where we really were.'

'Well, it's too late to go back on that now!' Max flung the contents of his wine glass down his throat before standing up and moving forcefully away from the table.

Abby gave a pained frown, a little surprised at his sudden anger. 'I wasn't suggesting that we should—'

'No?' he challenged, pouring himself another glass of wine. 'What is it you want from me, Abby? What do you want to know about me?' His eyes were glacial. 'Parents? Siblings? An exchange of the names of past lovers?'

The latter might be interesting. And painful. And destructive. She also very much doubted that Kate Mayhew would be included in that exchange!

She gave a half smile. 'I already know about parents and siblings from my research. As for past lovers—wouldn't that be a little boring for you, considering I don't have any?'

He gave her an impatient glare. 'Contrary to what you may think, I don't have that many either!'

Abby shook her head. 'This isn't very helpful, is it? Perhaps I should just leave?'

Max stopped his pacing to stare down at her frustratedly. 'Is that what you want to do?'

Yes! No! She didn't know!

If she left she wasn't sure when, or if, she would see Max again.

Max seemed to have the same doubts, taking a step towards her. 'Abby, I don't want to fight with you,' he groaned.

She swallowed hard. 'No…'

She had no defences when he took her in his arms—but then she didn't really want any. Held in Max's arms, being kissed by him, able to feel his response to her, she had no doubts whatsoever…

Doubts came later, much later, when she woke in the darkness of Max's bedroom early the next morning, her body still aching pleasurably from the intensity of their lovemaking.

She had been lost from that first kiss, their responses to each other wild and abandoned.

Too much so?

As if both of them had known they were trying to hold on to something so fragile it might break when exposed to the outside world?

There had certainly been no words of love from either of them. Just those intense hours of lovemaking, and Max cradling her in his arms as they both drifted off to sleep.

Max was still sleeping, she realised as she turned on the pillow to look at him. The early-morning light showed his face looking younger and less strained, with the darkness of his hair falling endearingly over his forehead.

God, how she loved him!

Enough to know that she had to be the one to leave this time. That if she stayed she would only do or say something she might regret—that she *would* regret. If Max wanted to take this slowly, to let time and familiarity decide whether or not they had a future together, then that was what she would have to do.

She slid silently out of bed, gathering up her clothes from where they had been thrown the night before and going into the adjoining bathroom.

Max was still asleep when she came back from taking her shower. She gave him one last wistful look before letting herself out of the apartment.

She was too restless to go back to her own apartment, and went to her office instead. There was something she needed to do before she saw Max again…

If the security man found her early arrival strange, he didn't say so, greeting her cheerfully enough as he let her into the building. One advantage of being on a weekly TV show!

The day before, after Gary Holmes's insinuations, she had impulsively got a copy of Max's show from two years ago from the archives, and then decided she didn't want to look at it.

Because it might confirm what Gary had said?

Maybe, but this morning, since she was alone in the building, apart from security, with no danger of being interrupted—especially by the gloatingly sarcastic Gary!—it seemed like the ideal time for her to sit and watch it.

As she had known it would be, it was distressing viewing. Rory Mayhew's despair was so utter that Abby's heart ached for him.

Those emotions dominated her first two viewings of the recording, but the third time she began to concentrate on other aspects of it—on Max's responses to the other man's rapidly escalating incoherency as Rory Mayhew seemed the worse for drink.

Max had obviously tried to direct the conversation under great provocation, tried to keep things under control. But when Rory Mayhew had produced an old service revolver that looked as if it might have seen use in the Second World War and started waving it about erratically, it had become obvious that the other man was beyond reasoning with.

His voice slurred from the alcohol he had consumed before appearing on the show, Rory Mayhew had begun to rant and rave about the things he was being accused of, the mistakes he had made, how they had cost him his career, the respect of his colleagues and his friends, and how he feared he was about to lose his wife and children too.

But never once during that tirade had Rory Mayhew accused Max of being involved in his downfall.

Gary's insinuations, she was sure, were exactly that—and, moreover, they had been made with the deliberate intent of driving a wedge between herself and Max.

She shouldn't have waited. She should have watched this recording yesterday, she berated herself impatiently. It didn't take away her uncertainties concerning the woman Kate, of course, but it did add to her impression that she and Kate Mayhew were not one and the same woman.

Damn it, she had been unfair to Max last night, and now she had left this morning without any word of farewell. What on earth was he going to think of her?

It was only nine-thirty now, she realized, after a glance at her wristwatch. Other people were starting to arrive in their offices. She could still go back to Max's apartment—maybe with coffee and Danish for their breakfast?

One thing she did know. She couldn't simply leave things like this between them!

The sun was shining as she walked back to Max's apartment. The birds were singing, the coffee and Danish she carried smelled delicious, and the prospect of being with Max again made her smile at the people she passed.

But the colour drained from her face as she turned the corner and saw Max standing outside on the pavement, talking to a woman just about to get into a car parked there. Because the woman, Abby knew without a doubt, was Kate Mayhew!

She easily recognised the other woman from the photographs she had seen of her, and her breath caught in a gasp of protest as she watched the other woman reach up and hug Max before getting into her car and driving away. Max's smile was wistful as he watched her leave.

Abby didn't even hesitate. She dropped the coffee and Danish into a bin before turning and walking hurriedly away, the tears falling hotly down her cheeks. There were no doubts left in her mind now, absolutely none, that the woman Kate was indeed Kate Mayhew. And, from the touching scene she had just witnessed, the other woman was still well and truly in his life.

'Why are you here, Max?' she prompted dully, her emotions still numbed by the scene she had unwittingly witnessed that morning.

After her abrupt departure she had been expecting a telephone call from him all day—had been prepared to deal with that. What she hadn't been prepared for was for him to actually come to her apartment this evening!

But she should have been, she realised heavily; Max had no idea she had seen him and Kate together this morning!

He looked at her frowningly. 'I was a little surprised to wake up this morning and find you gone…'

He would have been even more surprised if she had still been there when the lovely Kate had paid him a visit!

She shrugged, standing across the room from him, her shaking hands thrust into the back pockets of her denims. 'I was under the impression that was the way it was done.'

He gave a pained frown. 'I've apologised for my behaviour yesterday morning—'

'And your apology was accepted.' She nodded abruptly.

'But—' Max broke off whatever he had been about to say as his mobile began to ring, his expression one of irritation as he took it out of his pocket to check the number of the caller. 'If you'll excuse me—I have to take this,' he muttered, before moving into her kitchen.

His behaviour, in light of all Abby's unanswered questions, was like a slap in the face.

The caller was Kate, she thought instantly.

And then as quickly she chastised herself. Max must have dozens of friends and associates, family too, who'd feel comfortable telephoning him at eight-thirty in the evening. The caller didn't have to be Kate Mayhew. She was becoming paranoid, Abby acknowledged heavily. Believing everything Max did or said was somehow connected to the other woman.

She still had no idea what she was going to do about their relationship. Despite what she had learnt earlier today, and judging by his appearance here this evening, Max was obviously quite happy to let it continue. But she knew that she couldn't. Not under these circumstances.

She needed to know why Max had made love to her. Was it because the first time he had wanted to put a halt to their conversation about the woman called Kate who had called him? And the second time because Abby had been asking him questions about Gary Holmes?

Honesty had always been such a big part of her life. It was far too late for her to behave in any other way now. She could try simply asking Max for the truth about Kate Mayhew, telling him what she had seen this morning, but in reality she had already asked him about the other woman—several times—only to be told by Max not to go there.

'I have to go, Abby.' Max strode forcefully back into the room, his expression grim. 'Something's happened.' He ran a hand through the dark thickness of his hair. 'I can't explain right now, but—' He shook his head frustratedly. 'I have to go,' he repeated flatly.

'Okay,' she agreed dully, her gaze studiously avoiding meeting his.

'Abby…?' He grasped her arm as she turned away, one hand moving beneath her chin as he forced her to look up at him.

It didn't help. He looked so good, she loved him so much—and he was probably leaving her to go to another woman!

'It isn't what you think, Abby. Hell, I don't know *what* you think!' he ground out, shaking his head impatiently. 'This is what happens in my life—the way that it is. I receive a call and—'

'And you have to go,' she said evenly.

'Damn it, yes—I have to go!' His hands dropped back to his sides as he moved away from her. 'You've worked in television for a while now, Abby, in the media. You must know how it is—how my life has been for the last two years since I went back out as a political reporter. My stage is now the world stage, and when something of a political nature happens in it I have to go where it's happening. No matter what might be going on in my own life at the time,' he added heavily.

She gave a confused frown. 'You're saying that call was work-related?'

'Well, of course it was work-related. What else—?' Max broke off abruptly, his gaze narrowing on her with slow deliberation. 'You have been different the last couple of days, Abby,' he began slowly, 'and I'm pretty sure, knowing him as well as I do, that this change probably has something to do with Gary Holmes. Unfortunately, it isn't something I have the time to deal with right now.' He glanced down at his wristwatch impatiently. 'I have transport waiting for me, and I really do—'

'—have to go,' she finished for him, unable to hide the pain in her voice.

'Abby, when I get back we need to talk.' Max stood close to her again, cradling either side of her face with warm hands. 'Really talk. All I ask in the meantime is that you shut your ears to anything Gary Holmes might have to say about me.' His mouth tightened. 'I should have dealt with him long ago. I realise that now. This time he may not leave me any choice. Will you trust me on this for a while, Abby?' He looked down at her intently.

How could she trust him when she had actually *seen* him and Kate Mayhew together?

But not trusting him, she realized, now that she was with him again, didn't stop her loving him…

She had never felt so miserable in her life.

'I'll call you as soon as I can,' Max promised huskily, before his head lowered and his lips claimed hers with an aching need, sipping, tasting, as if he were committing the taste and feel of her to memory.

She didn't understand any of this. How could Max kiss her like this, be with her like this, if he really was involved with another woman?

Another woman he was even now leaving her to go to?

She pulled away. 'You have to go, Max,' she reminded him distantly.

He sighed. 'I wish it didn't have to be like this.'

So did she. But in retrospect perhaps this separation from Max was exactly what she needed to get back to her normal confident self; it was a sure fact that this relationship, a triangle she couldn't even begin to comprehend, was doing nothing for her whatsoever!

* * *

As she sat in her office the following day, eating a working lunch, watching the breaking news on television of a terrorist attack on the leader of one of the Middle Eastern countries—he'd been taken hostage—which was threatening to bring down the whole already shaky government, she wished that she and Max hadn't parted quite so distantly.

The voice of Max Harding—live coverage was unavailable at the time, due to the continuing unrest in the country—was informing her that so far there had been no ransom demand made for the kidnapped leader, and that the country was in turmoil as its citizens feared further action, possibly military reprisals, that would lead to all-out war in a country that had already known its fair share of death and destruction.

CHAPTER NINE

'You look terrible, darling.' Dorothy voiced her concern as she sat across from Abby in the conservatory of her home.

Abby gave a wan smile; even with the help of blusher on her cheeks, she knew that her godmother only spoke the truth.

But the last week had been the worst she had ever known—continually watching the news just in order to hear the sound of Max's voice.

The news from the war-torn country—the terrorists had executed the leader rather than releasing him, and the military were retaliating with force—was far from encouraging. But she had heard nothing from Max personally, and as each successive day passed her anxiety for him grew. The way they had parted and her unasked questions about his relationship with Kate Mayhew had faded into the background in her single-minded concern for his safe return.

In fact, her godmother's telephone call this morning to ask her to come over to the house had been a happy diversion of those worries. Although, looking at Dorothy's slightly flustered expression, she was beginning to have her doubts, sensing that the other woman wasn't happy with this conversation at all.

'Dorothy, has something happened?'

'Well, yes, darling. I'm afraid it has.' Her aunt sighed her obvious relief that Abby had introduced the subject. 'And Paul thought that the news might be better coming from me—'

'Dorothy, you're starting to frighten me now!' Abby stood up restlessly, her face pale. 'What is it? Has something happened to Max? What—?'

'Abby, calm down.' Her godmother looked deeply concerned at her reaction. 'He isn't dead, if that's what you're worried about.'

Well, of *course* it was what she was worried about. The country he was in was extremely unstable politically, and the fighting between the terrorists and the military had increased over the last two days. Max's reports had ceased altogether. In fact, there was very little news coming out of the country at all at the moment.

'Sit down, Abby—please,' Dorothy instructed briskly. 'Take deep, calming breaths, drink some of this.' She handed Abby the glass of water she had poured. 'And I'll tell you the little that we know.'

'Oh, God…!' Abby groaned weakly, her hand gripping the water glass so tightly she threatened to break it.

'I said he's all right, Abby,' her godmother insisted firmly. 'Max managed to get a message out through the television network there, who then passed it on to the English network, who passed it on to Paul, who passed it on to me, feeling it would be better if I spoke to you.' She drew in a deep breath. 'Apparently Max and his cameraman were caught up in some shooting a couple of days ago—he wasn't injured,' she added quickly, as

Abby paled even more, 'but the terrorists—wishing to play on a world stage, presumably—took the two of them hostage two days ago—'

'Two days ago?' Abby repeated disbelievingly. 'But there's been nothing on the news, nothing in the—'

'There's going to be. Which is why I'm talking to you before that happens,' Dorothy told her gently. 'After shooting the leader of the country, these terrible people obviously realised they had left themselves with no leverage. A foreign news crew must have seemed like a good way to recapture some of that leverage. There's going to be a news bulletin relayed later today, stating their demands,' she concluded heavily.

Abby felt sick. She couldn't believe this was happening. And she knew as well as the rest of the world how these situations usually turned out.

They needed to talk when he got back, Max had said. But what if he didn't get back?

'Drink some of your water, Abby,' Dorothy instructed firmly.

She did so without even knowing she had. 'What do they want?'

'What do they all want?' The other woman sighed. 'Freedom from tyranny in their given country, the release of political prisoners. It's never going to happen, of course. The military will eventually take control again, and put in one of their own as leader, and so it will all start again.'

Abby moistened dry lips, thoughts racing but going nowhere. 'And Max?'

Dorothy sighed. 'As I said, he's one of the people the terrorists are now holding as bargaining power.'

But the western world didn't negotiate with terrorists. Not now, not ever…

She swallowed hard, feeling as if her world had been turned upside down, and inside out; like everyone else, she had watched these situations before. But, although she'd watched them with compassion for the hostages' families, it had been in a detached way, never dreaming it would one day happen to the man she was in love with.

Did anyone ever think something so horrendous could happen to someone they loved?

'Abby, Max wanted you specifically to know that he's okay.' Dorothy came down on her haunches beside where Abby sat, taking one of her hands in both of hers.

She looked dazedly at the other woman. 'He did?'

'He did.' Dorothy squeezed her hand reassuringly.

'I— But— What about Kate?' Even in her complete shock she couldn't help but think of the other woman in Max's life, of what this might mean to her.

'Kate?' Her godmother looked puzzled now. 'I know nothing about anyone called Kate. The message that he's okay was for you and you alone.'

He was okay for the moment. Until the terrorists' demands weren't met. And then, as had happened so many times before, the killing would start.

Oh, God…!

The misunderstandings, the uncertainty between them, now seemed totally unimportant. Only Max and his safety mattered to her now.

And Kate Mayhew.

Because, much as Abby hated the fact, much as she hated the other woman's role in Max's life, she knew that she couldn't let the other woman just hear about this as a news item flashed on the television screen. That would just be too cruel after what the other woman had already gone through.

Someone had to go and tell Kate Mayhew what had happened.

And that someone would have to be Abby.

'I'm terribly sorry.' The other woman smiled at Abby blandly as the two women stood in the golden south-facing drawing room of Kate Mayhew's London home. 'I believe you told my housekeeper that your name is Annie Freeman?'

'Abby,' she corrected automatically, not so sure, now that she was here, that this was a good idea.

It had been instinctive, perhaps—the need to see someone, be with someone, who cared for—loved?—Max as much as she did. But here, in the quiet elegance of Kate Mayhew's home, with family photographs of before and since Rory Mayhew's death adorning every surface, Abby was having serious doubts.

The fact that Kate Mayhew was so startlingly beautiful didn't help.

The tall, slenderly elegant redhead had always looked lovely, of course—a beautiful accessory on her politician husband's arm—but the last two years, away from the public stadium, she had become even more so. The denims and T-shirt and loosely flowing red hair were certainly not anything she would have worn as the wife of a serving minister, and made her appear much younger than the thirty-five Abby knew her to be.

'Abby,' the other woman acknowledged, in the cool, well-modulated voice Abby remembered so well from their brief telephone conversation just over a week ago. 'Won't you sit down?'

'I'm fine, thank you.' Abby shook her head; this wasn't a social call, and—instinct apart—she didn't intend staying long. She would just say what she had to say and then leave. 'I believe we spoke on the telephone last week,' she added softly.

A flicker of recognition showed briefly in the other woman's eyes before it was quickly masked. She was looking at her guardedly now.

She was so beautiful, Abby thought dully. Absolutely stunning. And the thought that Max had been secretly involved with this woman for the last two years was heartbreaking.

She had to get out of here!

'Did we?' Kate Mayhew shook her head. 'I'm sorry. I thought you told my housekeeper that you're here in connection with my son's school…?'

It was the best excuse Abby had been able to think of at the time, knowing the other woman was unlikely to let someone involved with the media past the front door. Any more than she would have agreed to see a woman Max was possibly involved with. Abby wouldn't be here herself if she hadn't felt she owed it to the other woman not to let her just see the shocking news relayed over an impersonal television screen!

'I lied,' she told the other woman briskly, just wanting to get this over with now. 'I'm a friend of Max Harding's—'

'Who?' Kate Mayhew enquired with light confusion.

'Oh, please.' Abby really wasn't in the mood to play games. 'Even supposing the two of you haven't remained friends, you would hardly be likely to forget your husband's appearance on Max's programme shortly before he died—'

'I think you had better leave!' The other woman was breathing hard in her agitation, her face pale now, hands tightly clenched together. 'Abby Freeman,' she repeated. 'I realise who you are now. And, let me assure you, I have no intention of talking to a reporter—'

'I'm *not* a reporter!' Abby was just as angry, her nerves stretched to breaking point, sure now it had been a mistake to come here. 'I just thought—wrongly, it seems—that you'd like to know that, no matter what you might hear on the news later today, Max has got word out that he's okay.' He was still alive, anyway. And, really, that was all that mattered. Whether he came back to her or to this woman wasn't important. Only that he should come back.

The other woman was even paler now, sculptured cheekbones standing out starkly, big eyes a deep brown. 'I have no idea what you're talking about.'

'You will. Later today,' Abby warned her abruptly.

Those brown eyes widened. 'Are you threatening me? You get into my house under false pretences, talk about people I don't even know—'

'Don't be so ridiculous!' Abby was beyond patience with this woman now; Max was in danger, and this woman was continuing to deny she even knew him! 'I came here with the sole intention of reassuring you as to Max's safety. But, as you don't even know him, it doesn't really matter, does it!' Her voice broke emotionally. 'Just as it isn't going to matter to you if in the next couple of days he's shot and killed!' There were two spots of angry colour in her cheeks now. 'I'm so glad I don't have friends like you!' She turned on her heel and walked out of the room, out of the house.

And out of Kate Mayhew's life, she hoped.

'What the hell did you think you were doing?'

Abby blinked up at Max dazedly as he stormed into her apartment, his face furious, eyes glacial as he demanded an answer to his question.

Almost three weeks she had been waiting to see him again. Two of those weeks in absolute terror for his life as she recoiled from the awful photographs being shown of him and the other hostages on public television.

The English government had tried every diplomacy they could to secure their release without actually giving in to the terrorists' demands. And then yesterday, finally, the military had managed to overpower the terrorists—having put in place a leader who realised the benefits of a sympathetic western world—and release all the hostages still alive. Max—thankfully!—still amongst them.

Abby had first cried, and then laughed with absolute relief. And then she had cried some more. Her last twelve days had been an absolute hell of a different kind from Max's.

Something Dorothy had told her she looked like when she had come to Abby's apartment yesterday to tell her the good news.

She certainly wasn't looking her best now, she knew—a fact the make-up lady had fussed about four days ago as she'd gone about the business of repairing as much of the damage as she could. Although there had been little she could to do erase the shadows from beneath Abby's eyes from lack of sleep, or the hollows in her cheeks from lack of appetite. Wardrobe hadn't been too happy about the hasty alterations they'd had to make to her suit either, her figure having become almost wraith-like.

Max didn't look as if he had fared too much better. Very pale, much thinner than he had been, his hair in need of cutting.

He had never looked dearer to Abby!

But, after waiting in a state of increasing agitation for

him to come to her apartment once he was safely back in England—his telephone call from the plane had been necessarily brief—at least, she had thought it was necessary, now she wasn't so sure—she certainly hadn't been expecting his first words to be ones of attack!

She didn't understand. She hadn't been expecting hearts and flowers, declarations of undying love—she didn't believe that was Max's style at all—but neither had she been expecting this explosion of anger the moment he saw her.

'Abby,' he grated, hands clenched at his sides. 'I asked you—'

'I heard you,' she cut in forcefully, the strain she had been under, her lack of sleep, lack of interest in food, all finding an outlet in her own anger. 'I heard you,' she repeated more calmly. 'I just didn't understand you!' Her voice broke emotionally. 'What happened between your reassuring call from the plane, when you told me you couldn't wait to see me again, to what the hell did I think I was doing?' She shook her head, tears in her eyes now. 'You aren't making any se—' She broke off, staring across at him now as the truth hit her with the force of a sledgehammer. 'You've spoken to Kate Mayhew!'

He had arrived back in the country only hours ago, to cameras and reporters waiting to welcome the hostages home, and had endured a press conference since then—and yet somewhere in all that activity, Abby was becoming increasingly sure he had found time to telephone Kate Mayhew.

She sat down abruptly, her emotions in turmoil. She had thought—hoped—that Max's concern for her during the hostage situation meant that he felt something like the love she felt for him towards her. The fact that Max had obviously felt that same concern for Kate Mayhew, that he had actually already spoken to the other woman—been to see her first?—now gave lie to that hope.

'Well, of course I've spoken to Kate,' Max retorted savagely. 'You had no right to do what you did—'

'I had every right, damn you!' She stood up again, glaring at him, her heart breaking at how different this reconciliation was from her imaginings; it couldn't have been more different!

She had food waiting in the kitchen to be cooked, the table laid in the dining room—she had even put clean sheets on her bed! None of which, in the face of Max's hostility, were going to be used!

'You had been taken hostage, and the two of you are obviously…friends. I felt that the least I could do was go to her and try to warn her—try to alleviate some of the shock she would feel when she heard the news that day.' The same shock *she* had felt when she heard the news!

Max's hands were thrust into the pockets of his denims—denims that hung loosely on the accentuated leanness of his hips. The last two weeks had taken their physical toll on him: the dark shadows beneath his eyes, the deep grooves beside nose and mouth told of the emotional strain he had been under, not knowing from one moment to the next whether he was going to live or die.

Just looking at him was enough to make Abby wilt with weakness. She wanted to launch herself into his arms, to feel the living strength of him, just to know that he really was here.

He ran a hand tiredly over his eyes. 'Was that your

only reason, Abby? Or was it that you hoped to catch Kate during a moment of weakness, when she—?'

'Stop right there, Max,' she cut in incredulously. 'Do you have any idea of what it cost me to go and see her?' She breathed deeply. 'The two of us were lovers, and before you left you asked me to trust you; I thought my going to see Kate to reassure her of your safety was part of showing my trust in you. Obviously I was wrong!' She turned away. 'I think you had better leave, Max, don't you?' she said dully.

This was unbearable—unacceptable. She could only imagine what Max had gone through the last twelve days, knew only that *she* had felt as if she were poised on a knife's edge, not knowing if she would see him again, only sure that she loved him, longing to see him once more, if only to tell him that.

Now all she wanted was for him to leave—to go back to Kate Mayhew and whatever strange, unfathomable relationship the two of them shared and just leave her alone. She didn't want to be a part of their sordid triangle.

'Abby—'

'Go to her, Max,' she told him scornfully as she spun round to face him. 'I want no part of your relationship with Kate Mayhew!' She stared at him challengingly.

A nerve pulsed in his tightly clenched jaw. 'Kate and I aren't lovers—'

'No? That explains why you have women like me in your life then, doesn't it?' she retorted scathingly. 'I suggest you talk to *her* about it, Max— because I no longer want to hear anything you have to say!'

Uncertainty flickered in his eyes, his gaze searching now on the pale gauntness of her face. 'You look awful, Abby.'

'What a blessing for world peace that you never thought about joining the diplomatic service!' she said incredulously. 'Of course I look awful! I've been worried out of my mind about you—unable to sleep or eat.' She gave a self-derisive shake of her head. 'What a waste of time that was!'

He frowned. 'I heard that your last two shows have been incredibly successful.'

They had been. The ratings last week were the highest they had ever been. And she knew that for the most part she owed that to her worry over Max. It had brought her a new maturity, a seriousness that had completely obliterated that 'bright young thing' he had spoken of so scathingly at their first meeting, leaving in its place a quietly assured young woman who dealt with her guests with a new, forceful capability.

She was surprised that Max, only back in the country a few hours, would already know about that.

'They have, yes,' she confirmed abruptly.

'No more problems with Gary Holmes?' Max probed, his grey gaze intent on her face.

No more than usual. They obviously still disliked each other intensely, and Abby didn't trust the other man an inch, but Max being taken hostage and consequently being no longer in the picture seemed to have created some sort of hiatus in hostilities. The two of them just stepped warily around each other whenever possible.

'Not really, no,' she dismissed woodenly, wondering when Max would go. She needed to cry, badly, and she wasn't going to do it in front of him.

'That's good.' He nodded distantly. 'I— Hello, boy,'

he greeted Monty warmly as the cat strolled over to twine in between his legs.

Abby watched as Max went down on his haunches to stroke the happily purring feline, despite everything her heart aching at how good it was to see Max here, alive and well.

Their meeting hadn't turned out anything like she had expected—hoped—but the fact that Max had come back unharmed was more than enough. If he had come back to another woman it was something she would just have to accept.

And exactly *when* had she got to be so selfless?

The easy answer to that was—she wasn't! Even now she wanted to launch herself into his arms, to feel the physical strength of him around her, inside her, to reassure herself inch by precious inch that he really was safe, to touch him, to kiss him, to just lose herself in the wonder of having him here.

But she knew she wasn't going to do any of that. She had her pride, if nothing else. God, she really was starting to sound ridiculous now! Where was pride going to get her once Max had gone?

It was *her* Max had got a message out to. It was *her* he had—eventually—come to once he was free to do so.

But only, as far as she could tell, in order to protect another woman...

It was too much on top of everything else she had gone through these last weeks.

She bent down to snatch Monty up into her arms, holding him defensively in front of her as Max slowly straightened, his expression guarded. 'I really do think it's best if you leave, Max,' she told him huskily.

He took a step closer, then went very still—like a

tiger poised to spring. 'Do you?' he finally prompted gruffly.

'Yes!' She forced her gaze to meet his, determined to hold her ground; she wasn't sure she could have moved even if she had wanted to!

He shook his head impatiently. 'Look, Abby, even if I want to I can't explain about Kate. Not without—'

'I don't want you to explain about Kate!' she cut in forcefully. What new, fragile lover wanted to hear about a continuing obsession with another woman?

His mouth tightened. 'You just want me to go?'

Her arms tightened about Monty, a move he showed his disapproval of by squirming in protest. 'Yes.'

He looked at her frustratedly for several long seconds, eyes blazing, before giving an abrupt nod of his head. 'Have it your own way,' he rasped. 'This whole thing was probably a mistake anyway.' He turned on his heel and left.

But it needn't have been a mistake. If Max hadn't persisted in deceiving her about his relationship with Kate Mayhew... If she hadn't seemed to trip over the other woman at every turn... If Max had only loved Abby as she loved him...!

'If the sky were really made of marshmallow,' she told Monty emotionally. The saying was a favourite of her father's from when she was growing up and had wished for the impossible. Having Max fall in love with her was definitely one of those impossibles!

'I think I should tell you from the onset that Max has absolutely no idea that I'm here.'

Abby looked across the table at Kate Mayhew, still stunned at having left the studio on Thursday afternoon to find the other woman waiting outside for her.

It had been a strange couple of days. Only concentration on her work had distracted her from the heartache of having Max return safely only to show he cared more about Kate Mayhew's ruffled feelings at Abby's visit to her than he did the distress she had gone through.

To have Kate Mayhew come to see her, suggesting the two of them go and talk over an afternoon coffee in Luigi's, was the last thing she wanted. Or needed.

'Max who?' she asked the other woman dryly.

Kate Mayhew's mouth twisted. 'I deserved that,' she said huskily. 'I was—less than honest with you two weeks ago.'

Abby had known that then, and didn't need it confirmed now, but other than causing a scene and refusing the other woman's invitation, she felt she'd had no choice but to agree to this cup of coffee. A coffee neither woman had touched, incidentally. Luigi's frown was disapproving as the coffee cooled in the cups.

She shrugged. 'It doesn't matter.'

'It does matter,' Kate Mayhew told her, determined. 'I— At first I thought Max was different because of what had happened to him.' She shuddered. 'It must have been so awful for him, never knowing from one minute to the next whether he was going to get out of there alive!'

And Abby had lived every moment of that uncertainty with him. Only to have him return and berate her for visiting this woman…

'It would take much more than a few unstable terrorists to shake Max Harding.' She gave another derisive shrug.

The other woman looked at her with unflinching brown eyes, more lovely than ever today, her fiery red hair loosely flowing, her tailored black suit and cream blouse extremely elegant while remaining completely feminine, her legs long and shapely in high-heeled black shoes.

Next to her, in denims and a cropped white T-shirt, her hair secured untidily on top of her head, Abby felt distinctly scruffy.

'You're in love with him,' Kate Mayhew murmured huskily.

'I don't think so!' Abby gave a hard laugh, determined not to show how shaken she was by the comment.

'Oh, yes.' The other woman gave an assured nod. 'Is he in love with you too?'

Abby's hands clenched around her cooling coffee cup. She felt as if the breath had suddenly been knocked from her body; scenes like this were way out of her league. 'Doubtful, wouldn't you think?'

Kate smiled slightly. 'One never knows with Max.'

Abby shrugged. 'I'm sorry, but I can't help you there.'

The other woman straightened, eyes a candid brown. 'He won't talk about you, of course—'

'Of course,' Abby echoed dryly; he wouldn't talk to *her* about this woman either! 'Well, the fact that Max and I were once—friends has absolutely nothing to do with anyone but the two of us.' Any more, it seemed, than Kate's relationship with Max was any of *her* business!

'Max has been—different, since he came back.'

'You already said that,' Abby snapped. This really was beyond what any woman in love with a man who was involved with another woman—this woman!— should have to endure! 'But if you and Max are having problems then he's the one you should be talking to about them. Not me.'

'No,' Kate told her firmly. 'Max is very protective towards me. To the point where he wouldn't want to do or say anything that might upset me—'

'How commendable,' Abby bit out tightly; sarcasm wasn't normally a part of her nature, but she really didn't know how else to deal with this. 'Look, Kate,' she began again. 'If you've come here to warn me off Max, then I think I should tell you you're too late; we aren't even talking to each other any more! The truth is that Max and I had a—a mild aberration.' Her mouth twisted self-mockingly. 'But it was a mistake—for both of us,' she continued as the other woman would have spoken. 'An attraction that blazed fiercely and then just as quickly blew itself out. I'm sorry if that hurts you, but I can assure you it *is* over.' If it had ever really begun. Which, on Max's part, Abby was sure it hadn't.

The other woman sighed. 'I didn't come here with the intention of hurting you, Abby—'

'I've told you that it doesn't matter to me what you and Max do. It's none of my business. There's nothing between Max and I!' She was so angry with this woman, and with herself, but most of all with Max, for having put her in this position in the first place.

'Max isn't his usual happy self, Abby—'

'I've never seen Max happy, so I wouldn't know the difference!' She had seen him arrogant, mocking, and angry, but she couldn't say she had *ever* seen him happy!

But she had also seen him relaxed and charming, a little voice inside her head taunted. Over the lunch they had shared. And protective of her where Gary Holmes was concerned, gentle with the demanding Monty— and so sensually ignited the two of them had been in danger of going up in flames…

And none of that mattered a damn in the face of his obsession with Kate Mayhew!

The other woman shook her head, a haunted look in those deep brown eyes. 'I made a mistake two years ago, Abby—'

'I don't want to know!' she cut in forcefully, giving up all pretence of drinking her coffee and turning to unhook her shoulder bag from the back of the chair. 'I have no idea whether or not you intend telling Max about this meeting, but my advice to you would be—don't!' Her mouth twisted. 'He has a way of misinterpreting anything that involves me.' And she was already shaken enough by this meeting without having an enraged Max back on her doorstep!

Kate looked up at her as she stood. 'Of course I'll tell Max the two of us have spoken; we don't keep secrets from each other.'

That hurt more than anything else this woman could have said to her!

'He kept *me* a secret!' It was a cheap shot, completely unworthy of her, but in the last three weeks these two people, Max and Kate, had broken her heart. She didn't have to let them continue to do it.

Kate gave a regretful sigh. 'I really didn't come here today with the intention of hurting you—'

'You haven't,' Abby assured her abruptly. 'Goodbye, Kate. I doubt the two of us will ever meet again.' She turned on her heel and left, two bright spots of angry colour in her cheeks.

She had no idea where she went after that, totally oblivious as she wandered from shop to shop, not buying anything, not seeing anything, completely lost in her own humiliation.

Her only consolation was that this time Max couldn't blame *her* for what had happened. At least, he shouldn't. But that didn't mean he wouldn't. He seemed to hold her responsible for everything else, so why not this too?

Her telephone was ringing when she let herself into her apartment hours later, throwing her bag down in a chair to stare at the noisy instrument as if it were about to bite her. Max. It had to be Max. With the intention of hurling more accusations, no doubt. Well, she couldn't face them right now. She wished she had never set eyes on the man.

This should have been such a happy time in her life— one of those magical overnight success stories, that was really nothing of the kind but gave the appearance of being so. Instead she had met Max, and it had all become something of a nightmare.

She ignored the ringing telephone, walking straight past it to go through to the bathroom and run herself a hot, scented bath—always her point of refuge when she was troubled or in distress.

It didn't work this time. Her emotions were too much in turmoil. Part of her wanted to pick up the telephone and tell Max to get his girlfriend off her back, another part of her wanting to put even more distance between the two of them than there already was.

It didn't help that the telephone rang twice more while she was in the bath, setting her nerves jangling anew.

And then, on the fourth time of ringing, a thought occurred to her: Max didn't know her land-line number! She had never given it to him. It was an unlisted number, and the only time Max had called her in the past had been on either his or her mobile! Of course he could have asked Dorothy for it, but somehow she doubted it…

She left a trail of damp footprints as she jumped out of the bath, wrapping a peach-coloured towel about her nakedness as she hurried through to grab up the receiver. 'Yes?' she prompted breathlessly.

'Where the hell have you been?' Gary Holmes demanded angrily. 'I've been ringing you for hours.'

'What do you want, Gary?' she asked warily as she dropped down into an armchair; she'd thought she had made herself more than plain concerning the privacy of her home.

Although their working relationship had continued to be less than cordial these last two weeks, Abby had really been too numbed to react to any of the cutting remarks Gary had made. And over the last couple of days she had simply tuned the man out when he'd tried to ask her if Max would be appearing on her show now that he was back—as if. She'd been concentrating all her efforts on her work in order not to think about Max.

But Gary, of necessity, did have her home telephone number; it just hadn't occurred to her that he might be the one actually ringing her.

'What I want is for you to get yourself back in here now,' her director rasped impatiently. 'We have a change of guest for tomorrow evening, and a hell of a lot of work to get through before then!'

Abby straightened. 'What do you mean, we have a change of guest? Everything is set for Cameron Harper—'

'He's been bumped to next week,' Gary interrupted. 'It would seem that you've succeeded in working your charm, after all, Abby,' he added scathingly. 'Pat called me a couple of hours ago and told me that Max Harding has agreed to come on your show. Tomorrow night—

not for the last show, as you originally suggested he might.'

Abby's hand tightened so hard about the receiver that her knuckles showed white.

Max was going to appear on tomorrow evening's show?

No, that wasn't the question. The question was, why had Max, after all he had said and done, agreed—no, requested!—to appear on her show after all?

CHAPTER TEN

'I STILL don't understand what this meeting is about.' Abby shook her head slightly dazedly as she sat across the table from Gary in the conference room where they were all to meet.

Gary gave her a sneering smile. 'Sounds pretty simple to me.' He raised a sarcastic eyebrow. 'You practised your seduction on Max Harding. He fell for it. And now we're sitting here, waiting for the great man to arrive so that he can tell us what he's going to say tomorrow night.'

It was the last bit she didn't understand. Well, she didn't understand any of this, actually—least of all Max's *volte face*—but she really had no idea why Max wanted a meeting with Pat, Gary and herself at nine o'clock at night. It was going to be hard enough seeing Max again at all, let alone in Gary's presence.

'Hey, don't blame me.' Gary held up defensive hands. 'The great man dictates and we all jump!'

She didn't jump. Had no intention of jumping again. Ever.

And this was *her* show, and no one had even bothered to consult her on a change of guest for tomorrow

evening. Not a good basis from which she should interview any of her guests.

All thought fled as the door opened suddenly and the
energetic figure of Pat Connelly preceded Max into the
room. The small, rotund woman, in her usual sweatshirt
and joggers, her grey hair short and slightly ruffled, looked
slightly incongruous next to the tall, brooding Max, who
was wearing a dinner suit and snowy white shirt.

Abby's gaze instantly swung back to Pat as she swept
forcefully down the room to sit at the head of the long
table. But that didn't mean she wasn't wholly aware of
Max, as he strolled over at a more leisurely pace to take
a seat beside the older woman.

'Obviously Max needs no introduction,' Pat began
with irony, her homely face and less than sartorial elegance belying the fact that she was one of the most dy-
namic producers in television today.

'Obviously not,' Gary echoed dryly, his gaze, when
Abby glanced across at him, fixed challengingly on the
other man. 'What's this all about? Abby is all set to go
with Cameron Harper tomorrow—'

'I've already spoken to Cameron; he's more than happy
to appear on the next show rather than tomorrow—'

'What's the rush?' Gary interrupted his producer.
'Abby always had Max in mind for the last show anyway, so—'

'Max has offered to appear tomorrow, Gary, not any
other time,' Pat told him harshly. 'And, it may have es-
caped your notice, but it would be in our interest to pursue this while Max's recent—predicament is still so
fresh in people's minds.'

Abby was deeply aware that she and Max weren't
taking any part in the conversation. Not that it was too

much of a hardship for her; she would rather listen at the moment anyway. But she had never known Max to be less than verbally expansive. Especially when he was the subject under discussion!

She chanced a look down the table to where he sat, feeling a jolt of awareness as she found him staring straight back at her, those grey eyes hooded and unreadable, his expression grimly remote.

And as she continued to look at him—like a rabbit eyeing a fox—he raised one dark brow in silent challenge.

He knew about her meeting earlier today with Kate Mayhew!

Without his having to say a word, Abby knew that the other woman had kept to her intention not to keep any secrets from Max.

Well, that was just fine for the two of them. Abby just hoped that the other woman had also told him that *she'd* had no part in setting up the meeting—also that she had refused to discuss him, or their own brief relationship.

'It's done, Gary,' Pat was telling the director when Abby determinedly turned her attention and her gaze back to the two of them. 'So live with it.'

Gary scowled his resentment. 'I was under the impression this was my show—'

'And everyone else was under the impression that it was Abby's.' Max spoke at last, coldly, abruptly, making no effort to hide his contempt for the other man.

'It is,' Abby answered firmly. 'But I don't understand this any more than Gary does. You told me quite adamantly that you wouldn't appear on the show—'

'And now I've changed my mind,' Max bit out harshly.

Her mouth tightened at his sheer arrogance. 'And

now we're all supposed to get down on our knees and say thanks at the shrine of Max Harding?'

'Abby!' Pat gasped her surprise at the attack.

Abby ignored her, keeping her gaze firmly fixed on Max; there was more going on here than Pat could possibly know, and Abby didn't like the feeling of being simply a pawn in a game. Especially when she didn't know what the game was—only that Max was the one making the rules.

Max was looking at her with rueful respect now. 'It's okay, Pat,' he assured the other woman, without looking at her. 'Are you saying that you don't want me to appear on your show after all, Abby?'

He had her, and he knew it—knew that after what had happened to him in the last two weeks she would be committing professional suicide in not accepting the interview he was offering her. Especially if she wanted her contract renewed for another year. It wasn't *that* she was questioning, only his motives for doing this.

Why had he changed his mind now? The only thing that had happened since the two of them had last spoken on the subject that she could see was her meeting earlier today with Kate Mayhew. The other woman in his life…

A meeting, no matter what Max might think to the contrary, that had not been of her choosing…

Although she had no guarantee that Kate Mayhew had told him that when she'd confided that particular secret to him—any more than she had any idea what the other woman had told him about their meeting. If the coldness of his gaze was anything to go by, then it probably hadn't been anything good…

'…go over the list of questions Max has agreed to answer.'

She tuned back into the conversation as Pat put her briefcase on the tabletop and opened it.

'Now, just a minute!' Abby gasped, standing up. 'The list of questions Max has agreed to answer?' she repeated forcefully. 'Where is *my* involvement in that?' She was no longer looking at Max but concentrating on Pat instead. 'I'll end up as merely a mouthpiece—a bystander on *The Max Harding Show*!'

'Do you have a problem with that?' Max asked quietly, before Pat could speak.

Abby's eyes flashed deeply blue as she glared at him. 'I won't do it!' she said determinedly.

'Even at the risk of losing an exclusive?' he challenged softly.

Goading, baiting her. Which only made her all the more adamant. If Max had known her better—if he had known her at all!—then he would have realised she wouldn't be pushed about and bullied in this way.

'Even at the risk of that—yes,' she bit out tautly, her gaze unwavering on his.

The two of them continued their visual battle for several seconds. Max determined and unreadable, Abby stubbornly unyielding.

'Pat.' He finally spoke softly, his gaze remaining unwaveringly on Abby's. 'Would you and Gary mind leaving Abby and me alone for a few minutes?'

Every particle of Abby inwardly protested at such an idea. She didn't want to be alone with him, had nothing to say to him. But then, that wasn't the idea, was it? Max had something he wanted to say to her! And it wasn't too difficult to guess what that something was.

'Won't you sit down, Abby?' Max invited softly seconds later, when the others had left the room—Pat happily, Gary protestingly.

For once, Abby had found herself agreeing with Gary!

'I won't, thanks,' she refused abruptly, her palms feeling damp, her whole body aching from the tension she felt. 'If this is because of Kate Mayhew—'

'Let's leave Kate out of this.'

'I would be happy to!' Abby assured him heavily. 'But that's actually impossible to do, isn't it, Max?' she went on. 'Because everything you say and do begins and ends with Kate Mayhew! She came to see me today—'

'I know that.' His mouth was tight. 'She said that you refused to discuss our relationship.'

Well, at least Kate had been honest about *that*.

'Because we don't *have* a relationship!' she snapped, moving to the other end of the table, as far away from Max as she could get in the confines of the conference room, too distracted by his proximity to be able to think straight—except to know she couldn't allow the fiasco being suggested for tomorrow night's show to continue. 'Why don't the two of you just go public with your relationship, Max?' She sighed. 'It's been two years. The media can be extremely forgiving, and I'm sure with your way with words—' her mouth twisted scathingly '—you could arrange to bring all of this round to a romantic angle they will totally accept!'

'I'm sure I could,' he drawled. 'Unfortunately, that isn't the way it happened—isn't the way it is.'

'I don't believe you!'

'No, I know you don't.' He sighed too. 'But you're just going to have to trust me on this one, Abby.'

'I trusted you once before—I won't do it again!' Her eyes blazed, her face pale.

'No,' he accepted heavily. 'I can see that. But I *will* be appearing on your show tomorrow evening, Abby. And I *will* be answering the questions that Pat and I have already agreed on.'

'Pat had no more had a say in what those questions are than I did!'

'No,' he acknowledged without apology. 'However, the difference is she's enough of a professional to trust in my judgement.'

'And I'm not?' Abby guessed tartly. 'Fine, Max. Go ahead and arrange this between the two of you.' She snatched up her bag. 'But do it on the understanding that I may or I just may not turn up to ask you those questions on my own show!'

Max moved swiftly, grasping her upper arms, shaking her slightly in obvious frustrated anger. 'You are one of the most stubborn women it has ever been my misfortune to meet!'

She faced him unflinchingly, desperately hanging on to her anger in an effort to fight the weakness she felt just at his touch. A weakness that would leave her totally defenceless if she gave in to it. And at the moment those defences were the only thing keeping her from saying, To hell with all this. She didn't care what role Kate Mayhew had in his life, that she just wanted him. Here. Now.

How sad was that?

She shook back the dark curtain of her hair. 'More stubborn than Kate?'

He drew in a sharp breath. 'I told you—'

'To leave her out of this,' Abby finished derisively. 'Maybe I *will* turn up for the show tomorrow night after all, Max,' she said slowly. 'In fact…after some thought, I wouldn't dream of missing it!'

His mouth tightened. 'Abby—'

'Yes?'

He breathed heavily. 'I'm not your enemy, Abby,' he warned softly.

'No?' She faced him defiantly.

His mouth tightened. 'I'm really not.'

'I don't believe that either,' she challenged.

'We sound like two opponents facing each other in a boxing ring!'

'That's probably because it's exactly what we are.' She smiled humourlessly. 'And I should warn you—it isn't a fight I'm prepared to lose!'

Max looked down at her for several long seconds before releasing her abruptly. 'You're making a terrible mistake, Abby. I'm far from being your enemy, and tomorrow evening I intend proving that to you,' he assured her.

'Let the battle commence!' she scorned, before turning on her heel and walking out of the room. 'He's all yours,' she told Pat as she stalked by.

Because he wasn't hers.

And he never would be...

None of that iron control—thankfully—had faded by the following evening. In fact, it was the only thing that kept her from falling apart completely.

That and the professionalism that wouldn't allow her to become simply Max Harding's mouthpiece.

A fact he was shortly going to find out, she realized, after a quick glance at her wristwatch told her they would be on the air in only ten minutes. But on her terms, not Max's.

As usual she had arrived at the studio two hours ago. As usual she had allowed Make-Up to do their work.

Unusually, she hadn't spent any time talking to her guest, putting him at ease before they appeared live in front of the cameras.

She knew Max was at the studio too—had been informed the moment he arrived, an hour ago—but she had made no effort to go through her normal practice of chatting to her guests beforehand, establishing an ease, a rapport, before the show went on air.

What was the point? There was no ease or rapport between herself and Max. And there never would be.

'All set, Abby?' Gary appeared in the doorway of her room.

As set as she was going to be! 'I'm fine,' she said shortly, not particularly liking the feral grin on Gary's face, but knowing there wasn't a lot she could do about it. He knew she was angry about this interview, and he was loving all the tension in the studio.

'You're looking very—professional this evening.' He nodded his satisfaction with her appearance.

Deliberately so. This wasn't going to be like any of her previous shows. It hadn't been hyped as such by the television station throughout the day when they'd announced the change of guest, and Abby had dressed accordingly. The black tailored suit and white blouse were businesslike, her hair was swept up on top of her head, and her make-up was subdued—no lipgloss, only a peach-coloured lipstick, and blusher adding colour to the white of her cheeks.

'I have to go, Gary,' she told him woodenly as she received the signal for going on the air in five minutes.

'I hope you're going out there to get him, Abby,' he encouraged, blue eyes glittering with malice.

It gave Abby her first feelings of misgiving concerning what she was about to do. Anything that Gary could smile on so approvingly had to be suspect, she realized, with a belated flash of uncertainty.

Was it so obvious what she intended doing? That she had drawn up her own list of questions, and intended replacing Max's with them?

Was she doing the right thing? she wondered as she hurried to take her place in the studio.

Did she have any choice? came the second, heart-breaking question.

No, she didn't, she decided with fresh resolve. Max had his own reasons for agreeing to appear on her show, but they weren't *her* reasons. And her personal life might be in ruins, but that didn't mean her professional one had to be too. Max was playing with her—probably in order to continue protecting Kate Mayhew. He had made love to her for the same reason. And, while she didn't want to hurt the other woman, she didn't feel the same compunction where Max was concerned.

Her resolve was shaken even further when she saw Max waiting for her as she walked on to the set, and the colour—so expertly applied earlier—faded from her cheeks.

Max's eyes were hard, his expression grim. 'What are you up to, Abby?' he ground out suspiciously.

She gave him a startled look. How did he know? *What* did he know?

Her new set of questions had been prepared in absolute secrecy. How could Max possibly—? He couldn't, she decided determinedly. He was just guessing. As Gary had. The fact that both men had guessed correctly was more fluke than certainty. And bad luck for her.

She shook her head. 'I have no idea what you're talking about, Max,' she told him. 'Now, if you'll excuse me, I have to go,' she added firmly, as the theme for her programme began to play.

'Abby!' He reached out and grasped her arm in a vice-like grip, his expression intent. 'Abby, I love you!' he told her forcefully.

'How dare you?' she gasped, sudden tears blinding her.

Did he really think she was so stupid, so naïve, that she would fall for a ploy like—?

'I love you,' he repeated grimly. 'It's because I love you that I've agreed to come on this show at all. But there's much more at stake here than your pride or mine, and if you do this, Abby, then I'll have no choice but to fight back!'

She wrenched out of his grasp, drawing inside herself, her eyes no longer glittering with tears but with a fury she had no control over. 'I'll be waiting for you in the arena, Max.'

Pure professionalism took over as she stepped in front of the cameras, smilingly welcoming her audience before she had to introduce her guest for the evening.

The studio audience was buzzing, seemingly aware that something momentous was about to happen.

Just how momentous neither they nor Abby could possibly have guessed!

The interview began exactly as it should have done: Abby and Max were all smiles as they shook hands before taking their seats, and the first four questions were as originally planned, touching on the events of the last two weeks, with Max's replies relaxed and assured as he talked of the ordeal.

But the underlying tension was there nonetheless. And as Abby reached the fifth question of the evening she could sense a change coming over Max. Her resolve wavered once again as she hesitated about stepping from the script he had dictated for the evening.

Arrogantly. Arbitrarily.

No matter what he had just said, he most certainly didn't love her! He—

'So tell me, Abby,' Max suddenly drawled pleasantly, 'how are you liking presenting your own show?'

She stared at him even as she gave an appropriate reply. *What was he doing?*

'I hear rumours of there being a second series?' he continued lightly. 'You must be pleased by the show's success?'

He was attempting to take over the programme; that was what he was doing!

She straightened in her chair, her hands tightly gripped together, her pulse racing as she made the decision to step into the arena.

'I haven't heard those rumours, Max,' she said. 'But, to get back to you: this is the first interview of this kind you've given in two years. Understandably so. And I'm sure everyone watching this evening is aware of the events that led up to your decision not to appear in public again in this way.'

'Abby!' he warned softly, still seemingly relaxed with only the white knuckles of his hands, as he gripped the arms of the chair, to show that he was far from it.

'But it has been two years,' she continued evenly, knowing she was committed to going ahead with this now. 'And I'm sure we would all like to know—'

'Abby. Darling. I'm sure that you don't want me to tell everyone,' he cut in smoothly, 'that the only reason

I'm here tonight is because I could hardly continue to say no to coming on the show of the woman I'm going to bed with!'

CHAPTER ELEVEN

'AND that, my darling Monty, is when I hit him,' she concluded with an emotional sniff. 'And why I can never go out in public again. Never see any of my friends again. Never be able to face my parents again!' She groaned with remembered humiliation. 'They were watching all that, Monty. Oh!' She buried her face in her hands once again.

How could Max have done that to her?

And what had she intended doing to *him*? a little voice inside her head reminded her reasonably.

Yes, but that was different. He had *deserved* what she'd been about to do to him!

Besides, she'd had no intention of asking him anything to do with Kate Mayhew. The angry humiliation she felt at Max's hands—even seconds before they'd gone on air he'd tried to make her believe he was in love with her!—didn't extend to deliberately hurting the other woman or her children. Max had been her only target—and instead he had reversed the roles and made *her* the target instead.

She was finished—both professionally and personally. In fact, she would be surprised if she could find the smallest corner of the world who wouldn't know of her humiliation at Max's hands—and mouth!—by morning. Maybe Bolivia, after all? A loud pounding sounded on her apartment door.

Not happy with telephoning, with ringing her door-bell, now someone had actually managed to get as far as her apartment door!

The pounding continued, despite her efforts to shut it out, and through the width of two doors she could hear the muffled sound of a voice.

Max's voice?

She wasn't sure.

And she didn't want to be sure, reaching up to put her hands over her ears. Whoever it was would tire soon, would realise she either wasn't at home or she simply wasn't about to open the door. To anyone. Even if the building were to catch on fire. Like a captain, she would go down with the ship—

The bathroom door burst open. Abby's hands fell away from her ears as she stared at a wild-eyed, frantic-looking Max where he stood in the doorway.

Relief flooded over his features as he saw her gaping at him. 'Thank you, thank you!' he breathed deeply. 'Abby—'

'Get out of here!' she gasped, sinking beneath the rapidly cooling bubbles, not caring that this man had already seen her completely naked; that had been at a time when she had thought there was a chance the two of them might actually be in love with each other. Now it was just a complete violation.

But instead of leaving he stepped further into the room. 'I need to talk to you, Abby—'

'Well, you aren't talking to me here, damn it!' she

burst out incredulously. 'Besides, I don't need to talk to you. What I need, what I really need, is for you to just turn around and leave!' And never come back!

He paled slightly. 'Abby, please let me—'

'Please!' she repeated incredulously, sitting up slightly, the perfumed bubbles still just enough to cover her nakedness. 'You humiliated me this evening— deliberately, coldly, calculatedly humiliated me—and now you dare to say *please* to me?' She glared furiously at him. 'Get out now, Max, and don't ever come back!'

He shook his head, his expression grim. 'I know it must seem that way to you—but, Abby, I never meant to hurt you—'

'Oh, you didn't?' she challenged with sarcasm. 'Strange, because as I remember it that's exactly what you did!' Tears filled her eyes now. 'My parents were watching that show earlier, Max. My *parents!*' Her voice rose in horror at how they must be feeling after hearing publicly that their daughter had been to bed with this man. 'Don't come any closer, Max,' she warned, as he did exactly that. 'You— What's that?' she questioned sharply as she saw the recording in his hand.

'The rest of the show.'

'I don't need a hard copy of that show, Max—it's indelibly imprinted on my brain!' And on those of millions of others…

'I said it's a copy of the *rest* of the show, Abby,' he told her firmly. 'And you really do need to see it.'

'The rest of the show?' Abby repeated scornfully. 'There was no "rest of the show".' The last thing she had heard, before she'd ripped the earpiece from her ear and thrown it on the ground, had been Gary's instruction to go to a commercial break. Instruction? He had screamed the order!

'Oh, yes, there's a "rest of the show", Abby,' Max assured her determinedly. 'Put something on and I'll get this set up to watch.'

'You'll do no such thing,' she raged, very close now to completely losing it. 'Take your recording, and yourself, and just— How did you get in here, anyway?' she suddenly asked suspiciously. 'I know I locked the door.'

'Well, I didn't bother with the "it's your birthday" ruse.' Max sighed as he reminded her of her own initial method of getting up to *his* apartment seven weeks ago. 'But your doorman recognised me easily enough, and once I explained to him that you weren't answering your telephone or your door buzzer, that I was worried about you, he was only too happy to let me in with his key.'

'Oh, great!' Abby scorned. 'Now everyone thinks I'm a suicide case!'

'Not me,' Max assured her with a rueful smile. 'You're too strong, too courageous—'

'Oh, cut the bull, Max,' she said impatiently. 'After tonight the only way I'm going to be able to go out in public again is if I dye and cut my hair and change my name—and even that probably won't work!'

He gave an appreciative smile. 'The change of name we can discuss in a few minutes. But leave your hair exactly as it is; I happen to like it just that colour and style!' He sobered. 'Come and watch the rest of the show, Abby,' he invited softly. 'If you still want me to leave after that, then I will.'

'You most certainly will!' she assured him with feeling. But at the same time knew she no longer felt quite as desperately unhappy as she had.

She had no idea how, but a part of her—the part of her that was in love with him—somehow knew that Max was going to make all of this turn out fine.

Which was laughable after all that he had done!

She didn't have any clothes in the bathroom with her. Instead she put her robe on over her nakedness, its deep blue colour an exact match for her eyes. It zipped at the front from neck to ankles, meaning she was perfectly decent. Besides, what did it matter? Her inner emotions might have been publicly bared this evening, but Max had seen all of her bared!

He was on the sofa when she joined him in the sitting room, and Abby avoided his gaze as she deliberately sat in one of the armchairs. Monty, the continuing traitor, made no move to leave the comfort of Max's knee.

'I tried earlier to explain the situation to him,' she said dryly. 'But I guess he just didn't understand!'

'Oh, I think Monty understands more than you realise,' Max told her huskily.

Her eyes flashed deeply blue as she glared at him. 'He's a man,' she snapped. 'And men usually stick together, don't they?'

Max gave her a long, lingering look. Abby met his gaze unflinchingly. He gave a sigh. 'Let's watch the recording,' he suggested huskily.

'By all means—let's all watch my annihilation!' she agreed coldly.

Max looked as if he would like to argue that point, but instead he tightened his mouth and switched on the recording.

The first ten minutes of her show were exactly—painfully—as Abby remembered them. She had believed herself cool and in control earlier this evening, but the recording showed her to have been tense and obviously nervous, becoming borderline agitated as Max reversed the roles and began to question her, until, taking control again, she had begun to ask him about the events of two years ago.

She stood up impatiently. 'I've seen enough—'

'No—you haven't,' Max said firmly. 'Nice punch, by the way,' he complimented her dryly, as the screen showed him toppling backwards over his chair to lie unconscious on the ground, with a tearful Abby stepping over him as she marched out of the suddenly hushed studio.

It was almost worse viewing the incident like this, as one of the outsiders looking in. And the sudden appearance of an advertisement for a popular brand of nappies only made the whole thing appear even more ludicrous.

She gave a disgusted shake of her head. 'Couldn't they have found something with a little more—?' She broke off, frowning as the advertisement abruptly went off air and the cameras returned to the studio. 'What—?'

'Watch, Abby,' Max invited softly, his face grimmer than ever as his gaze returned to the screen.

She did watch. And listen. As had millions of others, presumably.

Gary Holmes, having left his control room, believing they were off the air, had confronted a still-miked Max as he slowly began to get up from the floor. The conversation between the two men had been both startling and enlightening!

'Satisfied, Gary?' Max challenged, standing to massage his painful jaw.

'Completely,' the other man returned scornfully. 'I

knew when Abby told me she was going to get you on her show that she was going to be trouble.'

'Is that why you've made her life such a misery these last months?' Max challenged.

'Of course,' Gary taunted. 'I tried to get rid of her completely, but that proved harder to do than I'd realised. Not that it matters now, because tonight she succeeded in totally humiliating both of you; what more could I ask for?'

'Kate Mayhew's continued silence, maybe?' Max suggested softly.

'Well, there is that, of course,' the other man derided confidently.

Max gave a disgusted shake of his head. 'I should have just let Rory Mayhew shoot you two years ago!'

Abby shot Max a startled look at this statement. What on earth did he mean? Rory Mayhew had gone on Max's show intending to ruin the man who was having an affair with his wife by committing suicide on his show. Where did Gary come into this?

'Perhaps you should,' Gary continued mockingly on the screen.

'You blood-sucking parasite,' Max told the other man coldly. 'Kate made the mistake of having an affair with you, and despite all her pleading you used it against her by telling her husband when his career was already falling apart.'

'Why not go for total meltdown?' Gary said, seeming horribly amused.

Max shook his head disgustedly. 'He was foolish. And so was Kate, for ever thinking you had any human decency inside you. But neither of them deserved what you did to them.'

'And exactly *what* did I do?' the other man challenged.

'You blackmailed Kate into continuing to see you by threatening to tell her husband of your relationship. And then, without telling her, you secretly blackmailed her husband with exposure, too. Doesn't directing pay enough? Is that it, Gary?' Max challenged. 'Or could it be that you did it for another reason?'

Gary gave him a scathing glance. 'And what reason would that be?'

'That you're a man who likes to have power over others,' Max said. 'You don't want to just stick the knife in, you like to twist it around too!'

'So I played a little game with the Mayhews that went too far. So what?' Gary challenged.

'It wasn't a game. It was people's lives,' Max returned icily. 'It cost Rory Mayhew his life and Kate Mayhew her husband—her children their father! Doesn't that mean anything to you, you bastard?'

'Not a lot, no.' Gary shrugged. 'Besides, you can't prove any of this, Harding,' he added dismissively.

'Oh, no?' Max challenged softly. 'Try looking at the cameras, Gary. See that green light? My live mike? Yes, I thought they might surprise you,' he said with satisfaction as the other man blanched. 'You see, I don't have to prove a thing, Gary. You've done that yourself—very effectively.'

Gary looked like a man who had been hit between the eyes, beyond pale now, looking almost green.

'I've waited two years for this, Holmes. I was never able to prove any of this before. But with your public— *very* public—confession…' He smiled. 'You're finished, Gary. Absolutely. Completely. In fact, I should think that in future you might have difficulty getting a job sweep-

ing the floor of this studio, let alone directing in it—'
He broke off as the other man, with a low, guttural growl,
launched himself at him, his hands going for Max's
throat, a maniacal light in those pale blue eyes.

'He was arrested seconds later for attempted assault,'
Max said. 'And I will obviously be only too happy to
press charges. The police are also going to look into the
events of two years ago to see if they can find any other
charges against Holmes—blackmail included—that
might stick.'

Abby sat in mute silence, completely stunned by
what had taken place in the studio after she'd left.

And the fact that it had been Gary—not Max—who had
been having an affair with Kate Mayhew two years ago!

And now? What was Max's involvement with the
other woman now?

'I felt responsible, Abby.' Max seemed able to gauge
her thoughts. 'It all came to a head on *my* programme,
culminating in Rory's death two days later.'

'He didn't get drunk and bring that gun on your programme intending to hurt *you* with it, did he?' Abby
asked wonderingly.

Max shook his head. 'Gary was always his target. But
there was nothing that he could do, that any of us could
do, to prove what Gary had done to all of them those
months before Rory's death. Yes, Rory made mistakes,
and, no, he shouldn't have got drunk and come on my
programme with his grandfather's old gun.' He shook
his head sadly. 'By that time Rory was totally irrational.
He had some idea in his head that shooting Gary would
put an end to all his misery. But once Rory sobered up
and realised what he had done, in front of millions of
viewers, I don't think he felt he had any other choice

than to kill himself. After that, all I could do was be Kate's friend and keep Gary Holmes as far away from her—and me—as possible.'

'And two years later I came along,' Abby realised weakly. 'Nosing. Prying. With Gary as my director.'

'And then *you* came along,' Max echoed softly. 'Beautiful. Impulsive. Warm. But with Gary Holmes as your director!' he acknowledged. 'He, as he's just admitted, was far from happy at the thought of my being a guest on your show.'

Hence his constant harassing of her on the subject, his deliberate attempts to drive a wedge between herself and Max—even to the point of implying to Max that the two of *them* had some sort of relationship!

'Your obvious anger towards me this evening suited him perfectly, Abby.' Max grimaced.

She raised heavy lids, her eyes pained. 'He knew all along I was going to switch questions on you.'

He shrugged. 'It wasn't too difficult to guess what you intended doing. Of course I couldn't have known what Gary was going to do after you hit me and walked out, but once he came down onto the studio floor and started talking—' He gave a shake of his head. 'It couldn't have worked out better if I'd planned it that way. Although Pat, bless her, must have thought I was completely insane when I indicated she was to keep the cameras rolling.' He gave a rueful shake of his head. 'I think the only reason she did so was because she was still stunned from seeing Abby Freeman lay Max Harding out cold on the studio floor! Where did you learn to punch like that, by the way?' He rubbed his bruised jaw.

There was laughter in his expression, but not malicious, or even full of the cynicism she was used to. 'My father,' she acknowledged, still slightly numbed by what she had just seen on the screen.

All this time—years—Gary Holmes had been largely responsible for pushing Rory Mayhew to the point of suicide. What sort of man was he? A very sick one, obviously.

But she must have really shaken his complacency— more than shaken it!—when she had announced she was going to have Max as the final guest on her show. The one man who, because of his friendship with Kate Mayhew, knew exactly what had taken place two years ago, but couldn't prove Gary's part in it.

All those times he had tried to keep her and Max apart—his sarcasm, his hints that Max was involved with Kate, in Rory Mayhew's death. No wonder he had looked so shocked that day at Luigi's when he'd seen Abby and Max together!

Until that point he must have been so confident, so sure that Max, with his well-known aversion to appearing on public television again, wouldn't even allow her access into his life, let alone actually be out having lunch with her. Hence his completely unexpected visit to her apartment later that day, and his broad hints that the two of them were involved. He must have realised that day that Abby was getting too close to Max, to the possibility of learning the truth about *him*.

Her gaze flicked sharply back to Max. 'I was never, ever involved with that—that excuse for a human being!' She grimaced her complete disgust just at the thought of it.

Max gave a pained wince. 'I know that better than anyone, Abby,' he reminded her. Bringing the warmth of colour to her cheeks as she acknowledged just how he knew that.

'There are other ways of being involved with some-one other than the physical,' she said tightly.

He gave an acknowledging inclination of his head. 'And you knew Gary in none of them.'

'How can you be so sure?' she challenged. 'You cer-tainly weren't a couple of weeks ago. In fact, as I recall you couldn't wait to get out of my bed and escape!'

'I wasn't escaping, Abby—I was running scared!' he told her firmly.

'Max, I saw you and Kate together outside your apartment that morning before you went away. I was bringing coffee and Danish for breakfast,' she added quickly. 'Not spying on you. And—'

'I never for a moment thought you were,' he assured her softly. 'But if the morning you're referring to is the one I think it is, then Kate had called in to see me on the way back from taking the kids to school. She had some good news to tell me—personal news. Abby, the mistake I made that first morning was in getting up and leaving the way that I did. But the fact is, I was— I've never been in love before!' He gave a shake of his head. 'I'm not, nor have I ever been, nor will I ever be, in-volved with Kate,' he assured her. 'I told you—I felt re-sponsible. At least, that's how I felt initially. Then I got to know Kate—and her children. She's a very lovely person, Abby—'

'I don't think I can bear to hear that right now, Max,' Abby cut in dully. 'I'm pleased for her—for both of you—that Gary Holmes has finally been made account-able for what happened two years ago. As you say, there's no way he will ever recover professionally from this evening. But I really can't bear just now to hear how wonderful Kate is—how—how much you care for her!'

That would just be too much, when her own life, both personal and professional, was in ruins.

'I told you earlier—not once, but twice, and again just now—it's *you* that I love,' Max murmured throatily. 'Abby, why do you think I finally agreed to appear on your show?'

'To try to get to Gary—'

'I told you.' He shook his head. 'I had no idea Gary was going to lose it like that. How could I have known? I came on your show, Abby, because I thought it was a way of showing you that I loved you. That my first public appearance in two years being on your show would convince the powers that be that I, for one, consider you a first-rate interviewer.'

'Is that why you threatened me earlier this evening?' Her voice broke emotionally. 'Because you're in love with me?'

'Weren't you intending to publicly crush me?' he returned challengingly.

'I wasn't going through with it,' Abby told him flatly, knowing that was possibly her worst humiliation.

She had sat there in the studio with him tonight, intending to hurt and humiliate him as he had hurt her, and in the end she had known she couldn't do it—that it would hurt too many other people if she did. So she had decided, in that moment of hesitation, to go back to the original set of questions.

'I wasn't going to do it,' she repeated firmly. 'Even as I started to ask you the question I knew that it wasn't the place or the time to air my private grievances. But, feeling threatened, you didn't feel the same compunction, did you, Max?' Her chin rose dangerously.

Max held her gaze with his for several long seconds

before reaching forward to pick up the remote control, pressing the button to resume playing the recording.

And, like a magnet, Abby found her gaze drawn to the screen. The studio was empty now of everyone but Max—Gary obviously having been taken away by the police. Apart from the bruise on his jaw, Max looked none the worse for the scene that had just taken place, and was every inch the seasoned television presenter that he really was.

And then Abby stopped noticing what he looked like and actually heard what he was saying…

'—to thank Abby Freeman for allowing me to use her show in this way to bring Gary Holmes's crimes, past and present, to light.' He spoke confidently. 'I'm sure you'll all agree with me when I say it's my misfortune that she *didn't* actually seduce me in order to get me on to the show. I should be so lucky!' He smiled ruefully as the audience broke into spontaneous applause. 'But any man can dream, can't he?' He gave a rueful grimace as the audience gave an appreciative laugh.

Abby stared across at him. With a few simple sentences and a certain amount of self-deprecation Max had turned her humiliation into something else entirely, making it sound as if she had been part of the whole thing, while at the same time making himself a figure of fun.

'Seriously.' Max's image on the screen sobered. 'Abby took a risk this evening, knowing she had no certainty of succeeding, and I would personally like to thank her. I'm sure that Kate Mayhew, if she were here, would want to do the same. What happened to her husband two years ago was a tragedy—compounded, as we've proved this evening, by the vindictive nature of one man. We've all made mistakes in our lives, and I'm in no way trying to exonerate any of the people involved, but those human weaknesses didn't have to end in the tragic way that they did. Tonight, I hope, has put an end to two years of personal speculation for Kate Mayhew and her family, and I'm sure that you'll all join me in wishing her and her children well for the future.'

There was another spontaneous round of applause.

'*The Abby Freeman Show* will return at seven-thirty next Friday evening, when her guest will be Cameron Harper. I advise you to watch out for the right hook, Cameron!' he concluded lightly, before the theme music began to play.

Abby stared at the screen as it went blank. Max had completely turned the situation round with a few well-chosen words, making Gary's behaviour two years ago the issue, rather than the fact that she had punched Max live on television.

She slowly moistened dry lips, not quite able to look across and meet his gaze. 'What happens now?'

'Well, as I said, Gary has been taken into custody—'

'Not to Gary!' She looked up protestingly. The other man had got everything he deserved!

'Well, for one thing Pat assures me that the executives are already clamouring to renew your contract.'

She swallowed hard. 'They are?'

'They most certainly are. And deservedly so. You're good, Abby—very good.' Max nodded. 'As for the rest— tomorrow morning's newspapers will carry both this story and the news of Kate's engagement and future marriage to Edward Southern, an Australian businessman.'

Abby's eyes widened. Kate Mayhew was getting married—but not to Max!

'It's what Kate came to tell me that morning you

saw the two of us together.' Max smiled at her stunned expression. 'She and the children will be moving to Australia after the wedding next month.'

And with her husband's death and Gary Holmes' involvement in it safely behind her, Kate was now completely free to move forward with her life...

'But I thought— I know you said— How do you feel about that?' Abby looked at Max uncertainly.

'In a word? Relieved,' he told her ruefully. 'After what happened on my programme I felt a certain responsibility for Kate and the kids. But maybe now, with Gary safely out of the picture for a while, we can all get on with our lives.' He stood up, moving towards her. 'And I would very much like my own future to include you, Abby. Do you think that's possible?' he prompted huskily.

She swallowed hard. Max had told her three times tonight that he loved her. In view of what she had just seen and heard on the television recording, was it possible that he had really meant it...?

There was only one way to find out!

She drew in a deep breath. 'I don't know if you're aware of this, Max, but my father is a vicar—'

'I wasn't, but I probably should have guessed.' He smiled. 'Although the idea of a pugilistic vicar may take some getting used to!'

'Wait until you meet my mother!' she warned, knowing her flamboyant ex-actress mother was the last person he would expect to be married to a parish vicar.

He tilted his head to one side. 'Am I going to?'

'That depends.' She moistened dry lips. 'You see, their dearest wish is to see me married to the man I love.'

Emotion flared in his deep grey eyes. 'Abby, are you asking me to marry you?'

Was she? Yes, she most certainly was! She loved him, he said he loved her, and she could imagine nothing she wanted more in life than to be his wife.

'If you are, then my answer is definitely yes.' Max cut in firmly on her thoughts before she could speak, standing directly in front of her now. 'I haven't mentioned it before now, but since I got back I've been offered my own current affairs programme, to be aired in the autumn, and as a married man I would be much happier being closer to home—and you. I love you so very much, my darling. I want to be with you always. I want to have babies with you,' he added huskily. 'Lots of them!'

She stared at him, hardly daring to believe, after all the trauma of this evening, that this could really be happening.

'Okay, I'll settle for two,' he conceded at her continued silence. 'And a guarantee that if either of them is a girl, your father will teach her to box. There are a lot of bastards out there—I should know—and I don't want our little girl getting involved with any of them—'

'Max!' Abby broke in laughingly, with relief as much as happiness. 'I love you so much. I want to be with you too, and we can have as many babies as you like!' Max's babies, with that thick dark hair and those beautiful grey eyes…

He reached out and took her into his arms. 'You never know—we may already have started on the first one…!'

That thought had already occurred to her too.

Wouldn't that be wonderful?

'I love you so very much, Abby,' Max told her intensely. 'So very much!'

And to have Max love her, to love him in return, was all the happiness she would ever want.

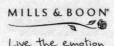

FREE

4 BOOKS AND A SURPRISE GIFT!

We would like to take this opportunity to thank you for reading this Mills & Boon® book by offering you the chance to take FOUR more specially selected titles from the Modern Romance™ series absolutely FREE! We're also making this offer to introduce you to the benefits of the Reader Service™—

- ★ **FREE home delivery**
- ★ **FREE gifts and competitions**
- ★ **FREE monthly Newsletter**
- ★ **Books available before they're in the shops**
- ★ **Exclusive Reader Service offers**

Accepting these FREE books and gift places you under no obligation to buy; you may cancel at any time, even after receiving your free shipment. Simply complete your details below and return the entire page to the address below. You don't even need a stamp!

YES! Please send me 4 free Modern Romance books and a surprise gift. I understand that unless you hear from me, I will receive 6 superb new titles every month for just £2.80 each, postage and packing free. I am under no obligation to purchase any books and may cancel my subscription at any time. The free books and gift will be mine to keep in any case.

P6ZEE

Ms/Mrs/Miss/Mr..........................Initials ....
BLOCK CAPITALS PLEASE

Surname ....

Address ....

....

..........................Postcode ....

Send this whole page to:

The Reader Service, FREEPOST CN81, Croydon, CR9 3WZ